The Walkaway Shoes

and

Other Stories

by
ENID BLYTON

Illustrated by
Andrew Geeson

AWARD PUBLICATIONS LIMITED

For further information on Enid Blyton please contact
www.blyton.com

ISBN 0-86163-927-8

This edition first published 1998
Second impression 1999

Published by Award Publications Limited,
27 Longford Street, London NW1 3DZ

Printed in India

CONTENTS

The
Walkaway Shoes

"You know, the two new brownies who have set up a shop in Toadstool Cottage make the most beautiful shoes," said Pixie Light-Feet to Limpy the gnome. "You should get them to make you a pair of shoes for your poor old feet, Limpy. Then you could walk well again."

Limpy went to see the two brownies, Slick and Sharpy. They bowed and smiled and welcomed him.

"Yes, yes, Limpy. We will make you such a comfortable pair of shoes that you won't want to take them off even when you go to bed!" they said.

Well, they made him a red pair with green laces, and they were so beautiful and so comfortable that Limpy went around telling everyone about them.

Soon all the little folk of the village were going to Slick and Sharpy for their shoes, and the two brownies worked hard the whole day long. They were pleased.

"Our money-box is getting full," said Slick. "Is it time we did our little trick, Sharpy?"

"It is," said Sharpy. "Now, in future we put a walkaway spell into every pair of shoes. Don't forget!"

Dame Shuffle came that day and ordered a pair of blue boots. "We've got just what you want!" said Slick, showing her a pair. "Try them on!"

She tried them on, and they fitted her so well that she bought them at once, grumbling at the price. "I'll wrap them up for you," said Sharpy, and he took them into the other room to find some paper. He slipped a little yellow powder into each boot and then wrapped them up and took them to Dame Shuffle. Off she went, and wore them out to tea that afternoon.

"Beautiful!" said Mother Nid-Nod, "I'll get a pair from Slick and Sharpy, too."

"So will I," said Mr Tiptap. And the next day off they went to buy a pair each. But on the way they met Dame Shuffle, who looked very worried.

"Someone came in the night and stole my boots," she said. "My beautiful new boots that cost so much. They are quite, quite gone."

"Oh dear – robbers must be about," said Mr Tiptap. "I shall be very careful of mine when I get them."

He got a pair of red shoes and Mother Nid-Nod got a pair of brown shoes with green buckles. Slick and Sharpy grinned

7

at one another when both customers had gone.

"Did you put the walkaway spell in them?" said Slick.

Sharpy nodded. "Yes, both pairs will be back again tonight!" he said. "And we'll put them into our sack ready to take away with us when our money-box is quite full."

That night the spell inside Mother Nid-Nod's brown shoes and Mr Tiptap's red ones began to work. Mother Nid-Nod heard a little shuffling sound and thought it was mice. She called her cat into her bedroom at once.

"Cinders," she said, "catch the mice in this room while I am asleep." So Cinders watched – but instead of mice running about he saw Mother Nid-Nod's shoes walk to the door and all the way downstairs, and hop out of the open kitchen window. How scared he was!

Mr Tiptap's shoes did exactly the same thing. The old man didn't hear anything, he was so sound asleep. But the brown owl in the woods suddenly saw a pair of

red shoes walking along all by themselves, and was so surprised that he almost fell off the branch he was sitting on.

"Who-who-who is that?" he hooted. "Is there someone invisible walking in those shoes? Who-who-who is it?"

But it wasn't anyone, of course. It was just the walkaway spell in the shoes sending them back to the two bad brownies. The people of the village began to get very upset. Everyone who bought lovely new shoes from Slick and Sharpy lost them in the night. And then, when they brought their old shoes to be mended and took them home again, those went too!

Slick and Sharpy just slipped walkaway spells in the mended shoes as well – and, of course, they walked away to the little

toadstool house the very next night!

"Our money-box is full," said Slick. "Most of the shoes we have made for the people here have come back to us – as well as a lot of their old shoes that we mended."

"Good," said Sharpy. "Let's go to another village now. We can settle in and do no work for a long time because we shall have so many pairs of boots and shoes to sell!"

"We'll just make this last pair of high boots for Mr Bigfeet," said Slick. "He has promised us five gold pieces for them – so that means we will have a lot of money from him and if we put the usual walkaway spell in the boots we shall have those, too, because they will come back to us tonight!"

Mr Bigfeet called for the boots that afternoon and paid for them. "I hope no one comes to steal these boots!" he said. "They're beautiful!"

Now, Bigfeet had a little servant called Scurry-About. She was a timid little goblin, very fond of her big master. She thought the boots were lovely, and she polished them till they shone that night.

"Oh, Master!" she said. "I hope no one will steal them!"

"Well, see that they don't!" said Bigfeet and went up to bed. Scurry-About always slept down in the kitchen. The boots were there, too. She looked at them.

"Oh dear – I sleep so very soundly that if anyone comes to steal them I would never hear!" she said. "I know what I'll do! I'll go to sleep wearing them! Then if a robber comes he will have to pull them off my feet and I shall wake up and scream!"

Well, she curled herself up in her small bed with the big boots on her feet. They reached right up to her knees! She fell sound asleep.

And in the night the walkaway spell began to work! The boots wanted to walk back to Slick and Sharpy. But they couldn't, because Scurry-About was wearing them. They began to wriggle and struggle to get themselves off her feet.

She woke up at once. "Who's pulling off the boots? Master, Master, come quickly, someone is stealing your boots!" she cried.

Bigfeet woke up at once and came scrambling down to the kitchen. He was most surprised to find Scurry-About wearing his boots. And dear me, what was this? They leaped off her bed, taking her with them – and then began to walk to the window. Up to the sill they jumped, and then tried to leap out.

But Scurry-About was still in them, and she screamed because she was stuck halfway through the window. "Help, help! The boots are taking me away!"

And then Bigfeet suddenly knew what was happening! "There's a spell in them!" he cried. "A walkaway spell, put there by those tiresome brownies – the rogues! Scurry-About, I'm going to open the window wide and let the boots take you away with them – but I'll follow close behind!"

"Oh, Master! Help me!" squealed poor little Scurry-About, and woke up all the

villagers around, so that they threw on
their dressing-gowns and came hurrying
to see what was happening.

Bigfeet opened his window wide. The
boots set off at top speed with Scurry-
About's feet in them, taking her along
too. Through the wood and into the lane
and down the street – and right up to
the front door of Toadstool Cottage went
those big top-boots!

And there they kicked at the door to be let in. Scurry-About was crying, and Bigfeet was shouting in rage. All the other villagers were calling out in amazement.

"See! They are walking off to Slick and Sharpy! The wicked brownies! Wait till we get hold of them!"

Slick and Sharpy heard all this and they were very frightened. Slick peeped out of the window. When he saw such an angry crowd he was alarmed.

"Quick, Sharpy," he said. "We must get out of the back door as soon as we can. Don't wait for anything – not even the money-box!"

So they fled down the stairs and opened the back door quietly. Out they went into the night and nobody saw them go.

The top-boots kicked the door down and everyone went inside the house. Scurry-About pulled off the boots, crying.

"They've gone," said Bigfeet, looking all round.

"But they've left behind their money-box full of money – and sacks full of the boots they made for us!" said Mr Tiptap, emptying them out. "Aha! It's our money because we paid it out to them – and they're our boots because they were made for us. How well-off we are!"

Nobody knew where Slick and Sharpy went to, and nobody cared. The villagers kept the boots and shoes and gave little Scurry-About two beautiful pairs for herself.

As for the money, it is being spent on a

birthday present for the little Prince of Dreamland, who is five years old next week – he is going to have a box of big wooden soldiers, who march away in rows – and then walk back again! You see, Bigfeet found the walkaway spell in a box at Toadstool Cottage – so won't the little Prince be surprised!

The Poor
Little Sparrow

Every morning James and Sylvia put out crumbs for the birds, and a little bowl of water. The birds always knew when the children were going to throw out the food, and they came flocking down to wait.

"Chirrup-chirrup!" said all the sparrows, dressed in brown.

"Tirry-lee, tirry-lee!" sang the robin in his creamy voice.

"Fizz, splutter, wheeee!" chattered the starlings in their funny voices.

"Pink, pink!" the pink-chested chaffinch shouted.

"Aren't they lovely?" said the children, as they threw out the crumbs and some crusts from the toast. "They really are friendly little things."

The children knew all the birds, though it was difficult to tell one sparrow from another. They knew the smallest one of all, though, because he had one white feather in his tail, and that made him look rather odd.

One day the little sparrow flew down with the others, but it couldn't seem to stand on the ground properly. It fell over, then tried to stand upright again, and then fell over again.

"Look at the poor little sparrow," said Sylvia, who was very tender-hearted. "What's the matter with it? It can't stand."

"It's hurt its leg," said James. "Oh, Sylvia – I believe its leg is broken. Can you see?"

Sylvia went slowly closer to the birds. They did not mind, for they trusted the two children. "Oh, James, you are right," she said. "Its leg *is* broken. Whatever are we to do?"

Now that morning the poor little sparrow had been caught by a cat, but had managed to get away. Its little leg

had been broken, and the tiny creature did not know why it could not stand properly, nor why it was in pain. It had joined the other birds as usual for its breakfast, but it could not eat for it felt too ill.

Suddenly it fell right over and lay on the grass. Its eyes closed. Sylvia picked it up gently and put its soft little head against her cheek.

"Poor little sparrow," she said. "It says in the Bible that God sees every sparrow that falls, so I expect He saw you too, and hoped I would pick you up. Well, I have – but I don't know what to do to make you better."

But her mother knew. As soon as she saw the little bird she took out the old, empty, canary's cage and put the sparrow on to some clean sand at the bottom of the cage.

"It has had a shock," said their mother. "It will come awake soon, and will be all right. Oh, look! Its leg is broken!"

"How can we mend it?" asked Sylvia, almost in tears.

"Well," said her mother, "if we break our legs the doctor sets the bone in the right position, and then ties it to something that will keep it straight till the broken bone joins together and grows properly again. What can we tie to the sparrow's tiny leg to keep it straight?"

"A match – a match!" cried James, and he emptied some out of a box.

"That's a good idea," said Mother.

She gently picked up the sparrow, whose eyes were still closed, and laid it on the table. Then she tried to set the poor little leg straight. With strands of silk she fastened the straight matchstick to the

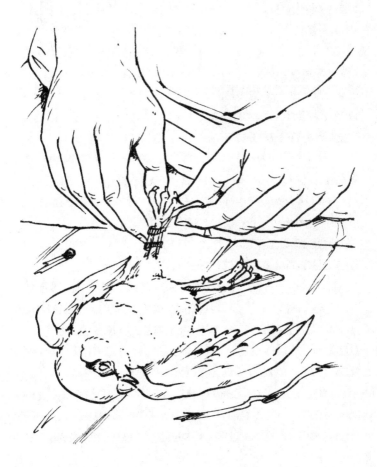

thin, small leg. It looked very strange – but now the broken leg was straight again.

"Oh, Mummy," said Sylvia joyfully, "you've done it so nicely. When the bone joins again, the leg will be quite all right, won't it?"

"I hope so," said her mother, putting the sparrow into the cage and shutting the door. "We shall keep the tiny thing in here, and feed it until the leg is quite right and then it shall go free again."

When the sparrow opened its eyes it was surprised to find itself in a cage. Its leg still felt strange, but it now no longer fell over, because the matchstick supported it. The little bird flew to a perch and chirruped.

James gave it some seed. Sylvia gave it a mixture of potato and breadcrumbs, and the sparrow was simply delighted. It had a little dish of water for a bath and another dish to drink from, set at the side of the big cage. At first it fluttered its wings against the bars of the cage to get out, for it hated not being free. But, as it

still did not feel very well, it soon gave up struggling and sat contentedly on a perch, feeding and bathing whenever it wanted to.

The leg healed quickly. It was marvellous to see it. The skin joined nicely, and the broken bone seemed to grow together at once.

"I think we might let our little sparrow fly away now," said their mother one day. "I am sure his leg is all right."

"Are you going to take the matchstick off now?" asked Sylvia.

"Yes," said her mother. So she took hold of the half-frightened bird, and carefully and gently took away the silk binding from the leg and match. The match fell off – and the little leg was as straight and strong as ever.

"We've mended its leg! We've mended its leg!" shouted the children in delight. "You aren't a poor little sparrow any more. Fly away, fly away!"

The sparrow gave a chirrup and flew straight out of the window. How glad it was to be out of the cage! It flew into the trees, and chirruped so loudly that all the other sparrows came round to hear what it had to say.

Now you would not think that a small sparrow could possibly help the children in anything, would you? And yet, a few weeks later, a very strange thing happened.

James and Sylvia had some glass marbles, the prettiest things you ever saw. They were blue and green and pink, and had white lines curving through

them. James and Sylvia were very proud of them, for they had belonged to their father.

"You can't get marbles like these nowadays," said Father. "Take care of them."

Well, James and Sylvia took them to play with in the fields, and there they met David, a big rough boy whom none of the children liked. When he saw the marbles he came up.

"Give me those," he said, "and I'll give you some of mine."

"No, thank you," said James, gathering his marbles up quickly. But he wasn't quick enough. David grabbed some of them and ran off laughing. Sylvia and James went after him.

"They are our marbles!" shouted James. "Give them back, David!"

"I'll put them somewhere and you take them," called back David – and what do you suppose he did with them? Why, the horrid boy dropped them all into a hole in a tree. Then he ran off, giggling.

James and Sylvia ran to the tree. They

tried to slip their small hands into the hole but they couldn't. The hole was too small.

"We can't get our marbles out," said Sylvia. "They're gone. Oh, that horrid boy!"

"Chirrup!" said a cheerful little voice nearby. The children looked up. It was their little sparrow. They knew it was the same one because of the white feather in his tail.

"I wish you could get our marbles," sighed James. "Your foot is quite small enough to go into the hole, Sparrow."

"Chirrup!" said the sparrow – and what do you think he did? Why, he flew to the hole, and instead of putting in his foot, he put the whole of himself in. Yes, he quite disappeared into that little hole – but not for long.

He popped up again, head-first – and in his beak he held a green marble. He dropped it on to the ground and disappeared into the hole once more. Up he came, with a blue marble this time. The children were so astonished that

they didn't even pick up the marbles.

The little sparrow fetched every single marble out of the hole before he flew off with a last cheerful chirrup. Then the children picked them up, and went racing home to tell their mother the strange and lovely happening.

"How very extraordinary!" she said. "It must be put into a story, for everyone will love to read about the poor little sparrow that did such a kind thing. It just shows what friends we can make, if only we are kind to even the smallest things."

So here is the story – and I do hope you enjoyed it.

Oh,
Sammy!

People were always saying "Oh, Sammy!" to Sammy. He did such silly things. Once he put on his dirty jersey and his clean jersey too, and his mother hunted all the morning for the dirty one because she wanted to wash it. But Sammy was wearing them both at school, feeling very hot and wondering why.

Once his teacher told him to sharpen his pencils, and Sammy took the pens instead, and tried to sharpen all the ends. And another time the teacher told him to fill up the flower vase with water from the jug, and Sammy took the wrong jug by mistake and put orange squash into all the jars and bowls.

He really was a silly little boy, and it was no wonder that people kept saying

"Oh, Sammy!" to him. They said it in surprise. They said it in rage. They said it in sadness, to think that a boy should be so silly.

But Sammy didn't bother much. He just looked at everyone and said "Sorry!" But he never seemed to try to do better.

Now one day his teacher planned a treat for all his boys. "We will take the day off tomorrow," said kind Mr Brown. "The weather is so fine now. Bring sandwiches to school with you, a swimming costume and a towel, and money for bus fares and a drink."

"Ooooh!" said all the boys, excited. Sammy especially was pleased, because he was a good swimmer, and there was nothing he liked more than swimming and diving.

"Take your homework down now," said Mr Brown. "I shall, of course, expect you to do a good deal of work tonight at home, to make up for missing school tomorrow. But I am sure you won't mind that."

"Of course not, sir!" said all the boys,

and they began to write down what they were to do for homework. They had to do sums, which they wrote down carefully, copying them from the blackboard. They had to learn to spell a list of words. They had to learn a long piece of poetry, which they also copied down from the blackboard.

"Everything down in your note-books?" asked Mr Brown. "That's good.

Now please remember – any boy who shirks his homework tonight will not go with us tomorrow. I expect good work from you in return for a treat."

"Of course, sir," said the boys, and they all made up their minds to do their very, very best.

"Does anyone pass by old Mr Jones's house?" asked Mr Brown, as the boys began to pack up their things. "I want someone to take a note to him."

"I pass his house, sir," said Sammy. "I'm the only one that goes that way. All the others go the opposite way; I'll take it, sir."

"Thank you, Sammy," said Mr Brown. Sammy took the envelope and put it into his pocket. Off he went home, his homework notebook in his other pocket. Sammy meant to do some marvellous work that night just to show Mr Brown how glad he was to have a day's holiday the next morning.

Sammy came to old Mr Jones's house. He rang the bell. Nobody came – but in the hall a little dog barked and growled.

"Bother!" said Sammy. "I believe Mr Jones is out." He knocked loudly and the little dog inside nearly went mad with rage.

"Bark and growl all you like," said Sammy. "I've only come to bring a note for your master."

Nobody answered the door. There was nobody in but the dog. "Well, I must put the note through the letterbox, that's all," said Sammy, and slipped his hand into the wide brass letterbox.

Then he went home. He had tea and told his mother all about the treat for the next day. "I'm going to do a good evening's work," he said, and settled down at the table. He put his hand into his pocket to take out his homework notebook – but instead he pulled out the envelope for Mr Jones!

How very extraordinary! What was the note doing in his pocket? Surely he had put it into Mr Jones's letterbox! Quickly, Sammy hunted through his pockets for his homework notebook. It wasn't there!

"Mum! Oh, Mum! I've posted my notebook through Mr Jones's letterbox, instead of the letter that Mr Brown gave me!" wailed Sammy. "Mum, what am I to do? I must do my homework tonight. It's the treat tomorrow."

"Oh, Sammy!" said his mother, as she had said a thousand times before. "Oh, Sammy!" She stared at him in dismay. Why did Sammy do these silly things? "Well," she said, "you must go back to Mr Jones's house and see if he's home yet, that's all. Then you can give him the note and ask him for your notebook back."

"Yes, I'll do that," said Sammy, cheering up. "I expect he's back by now." He raced off to Mr Jones's house. He rang and he knocked, but the only answer he got was the barking of the furious little dog inside.

"Oh dear – he's not back yet," said poor Sammy. "Well – I must wait, that's all."

So he sat down on the front doorstep and waited for Mr Jones to come home. He waited and he waited. The little dog barked and growled. Mr Jones didn't come.

Six o'clock struck from the church

tower. Seven o'clock struck. This was dreadful! Sammy was tired and worried. Oh, Mr Jones, do come!

Then, at almost half past seven, old Mr Jones came walking briskly up the street. He was most surprised to see Sammy on his doorstep.

"Please, Mr Jones," said Sammy, "Mr Brown gave me a note for you – but by mistake I put my homework notebook into your letterbox. So I've been waiting here for you to come home so that you could open your door and give it to me."

"Oh, Sammy! Whatever will you do next?" said Mr Jones, with a laugh. He opened the door, and Sammy stooped to get his notebook. The little dog stared at him, barking. "Down, Tinker, down!" said Mr Jones, sternly.

Then what a shock there was for poor Sammy! Tinker had torn his notebook into rags! Every page had been nibbled and chewed. Poor Sammy couldn't read what he had written there that morning. His notebook was nothing but scraps of torn paper.

He burst into tears and ran home. It was getting dark now, and his mother was worried about him. He ran into the house and sobbed out the tale of the torn notebook. "Mum! I must go round to Tim's or Peter's, and copy down from their notebook what my homework is," he said.

"It's too late to do that now," said his mother. "You ought to have thought of that before. I will write a note to explain to Mr Brown tomorrow."

She did – but when Mr Brown read it, he shook his head and frowned. "I'm

sorry about this, Sammy," he said. "But I can't excuse your homework today – you see, it was because of your own silliness that it isn't done. Silliness is just as bad as carelessness or laziness. Just as bad. So I'm afraid, my boy, you must stay here at school and do your homework, while we go off for our picnic."

"Oh, Mr Brown!" said Sammy, nearly in tears.

"Oh, Sammy!" said Mr Brown. "Now sit down and begin, Sammy. When you have finished, catch the bus and join us – but finish all your work first. And Sammy – don't let your silliness rob you of any treat in the future!"

"I won't, I won't," said Sammy, sitting down and looking at the blackboard. "I know it's not you that's punishing me, Mr Brown. I know it's my own silly self. I couldn't stop you punishing me, if you wanted to – but I can stop myself, can't I?"

"Yes – if you want to hard enough!" said Mr Brown. "Well – goodbye! Perhaps we shall see you later in the day!"

He did – because Sammy did two hour's hard work, and then caught the bus. He missed a good deal of the treat, but he did have some of it! And do you know, Sammy is quite glad he had to miss some of it. Because, you see, it gave him a shock and taught him a lesson.

"And now," says Sammy, "I shan't be silly any more!"

The Tail of
Bup the Bunny

There was once a bunny called Bup. He was very vain and longed for everyone to look at him and admire him. His whiskers were long, his ears were big, and his fur was thick. The only thing he didn't like was his tail.

It was just a furry blob, like all rabbits' tails. But Bup wanted a big tail, one like Bushy the squirrel's, or a long one like Puss Cat's. It was horrid to have a little bobtail that nobody took any notice of at all.

Then, one day, when he was out in the woods, he found a lovely long white tail. It had belonged to a toy cat that a little boy had taken for a walk. The tail had caught in a bramble and fallen off, so the little boy had left it there.

Bup picked it up and looked at it. Here was exactly the kind of tail he had so often wanted. He would take it home, try it on, and see how it looked!

So off he went, *clippitty-clippitty* through the wood, and ran down his hole. When he was safely down there, he tied the long white tail on to his own, and then looked over his shoulder to see what it was like.

"My!" he said. "I look grand! Yes, I do! I shall have this tail for my own, and pretend to everyone that it is real. No one will know, and they will all admire me and be jealous! I shall be the only rabbit with a long tail!"

He stayed in his hole for a few days, and when his friends came to see what was the matter, he put his head out and answered them very proudly.

"I am growing a long tail," he said. "I hear it's quite the fashion now. It's only half-grown yet, but as soon as it is full-grown, I'll show it to you."

Well, all the rabbits were most astonished. They asked each other whether anyone had heard of a long-tailed bunny before, but no one ever had. They began to think that Bup was making fun of them, so they waited anxiously for the day to come when he would come and play with them again.

On the seventh day Bup the bunny came out of his hole. He had tied on the toy cat's tail very firmly, so that it quite hid his own bobtail. As he lolloped out of his hole, all the rabbits cried out in surprise.

"Yes, he's grown a long tail! Yes, he has! Come and look, everybody! Bup has a long tail!"

Not only the rabbits came to see, but the foxes and weasels, sparrows and thrushes, hedgehogs and moles. The foxes and weasels were not allowed to come too near, for the rabbits hated them, but they came quite near enough to see the wonderful long tail.

How proud Bup was! He hopped about here and there, showing off his long tail, enjoying all the cries of surprise and envy.

"How did you do it, Bup?" asked the other rabbits. "Tell us, and we will do the same."

Bup knew quite well that they couldn't do the same because his was only a pretend tail. But he couldn't tell them that, of course, so he sat down and looked very wise.

"All you've got to do," he said, "is to sit at home in your burrow, think about tails for seven days, and then at the end of

that time you will have one as good as
mine."

Well, the silly rabbits believed him! Off
they all went to their burrows, and sat at

home for seven days thinking of nothing but tails. But alas for them! When they came out again their tails were as short as ever! They were dreadfully disappointed.

"You are stupid creatures," said Bup, curling his whiskers. "I am the cleverest of all of you. Why don't you make me your king? It would be nice for you to have a long-tailed rabbit for a king, wouldn't it?"

Now, not many rabbits liked Bup, for he was so vain. But he was so determined to be king that at last they thought they had better make him their chief.

So they all set out to go to Breezy Hill where they held their important meetings. They sat round in a ring, with Bup in the middle and the oldest rabbit by him.

"Friends," said the oldest rabbit. "You are met together today to decide whether Bup the bunny shall be your king or not. He is the only long-tailed rabbit in our town. We have all tried to grow tails like his and we cannot. Therefore it seems

as if he must be the cleverest among us.
Shall we make him king?"

But before the listening rabbits could
answer, a red fox came slinking up. He
had smelled the rabbits from far off, and
had come to see if he could pick one of
them up for his dinner. They saw him
coming over the hilltop, and with one
frightened look they took to their heels
and fled.

Bup fled too. His long tail dragged on the ground behind him, but he had forgotten all about it. All he thought of was his hole, his lovely, safe, cosy hole! If only he could get there before the red fox caught him!

The fox chose to chase Bup, for he was fat and could not run quite so fast as the others. So off he went after poor Bup.

All the other rabbits reached their holes safely, and popped their heads out to watch the race. Nearer and nearer the fox came till he was almost on top of Bup. Then he suddenly made a snatch at the rabbit's long tail – and got it in his mouth!

"Oh! Oh! Now Bup is caught!" cried all the watching rabbits.

But the string that tied the long tail on to Bup suddenly broke, and Bup raced on free, while the astonished fox stopped still with the tail in his mouth.

"My! Oh my!" sang out the rabbits. "Why, Bup's got a short tail as well as a long tail! Just look! There's his little bobtail, just like ours!"

So there was, quite plain to see, as Bup ran helter-skelter for his hole. Down he popped in safety, and lay there panting. How glad he was that his long tail had only been a pretend one!

The fox gave one chew at the pretend tail and then blew it out of his mouth. Off he went in disgust. When he was safely out of sight, the rabbits all came crowding out to see the tail. They soon found out that it was nothing but a toy cat's tail, and how cross they were!

"To think that we all sat in our burrows for seven days, thinking of nothing but tails!" cried the oldest rabbit. "And we nearly made that wicked rabbit our king!"

"And how foolish we should have been if we had grown long tails!" said another. "Why, the fox would catch us easily if our tails were any longer!"

"Where's that stupid Bup Bunny?" cried all the rabbits. "Let us go and find him!"

So off they went to Bup's burrow and dragged him out. They gave him a good scolding so that both his ears drooped, and his eyes filled with tears.

And that was the end of Bup being so vain. If ever he showed any signs of being proud again, someone would say to him,

"Well, Bup? Have you grown another long tail yet?"

And then Bup would go very red and run away!

The
Clockwork Mouse

There was once a little boy called Gerry, who was very kind to his toys. He didn't break them. He didn't leave them out in the rain. He really did look after them and love them. So they loved him too. But most of all the clockwork mouse loved Gerry. You see, the clockwork mouse had once lost his key, so he couldn't be wound up, and that made him very unhappy. He did so love to run about, and if he wasn't wound up he couldn't.

Nobody ever knew how he lost his key. It just disappeared. The monkey thought that it might have dropped out on the floor and been sucked up in the vacuum cleaner.

"Then it would go into the dustbin with the rubbish," said the teddy. "And that would be the end of it."

Then Gerry noticed that the mouse hadn't a key. "Where's your key?" he said. "I'll wind you up and give you a run."

The mouse looked sadly up at him. He couldn't have a run round the floor, looking for crumbs, because his key was lost.

"Why, your key is gone!" said Gerry, and he hunted about for it. But he

couldn't find it. "Never mind," said Gerry. "I'll do something about it, Mouse. I can see by your face that you feel sad about it. I know how I should feel if I could only run when I was wound up – and suddenly lost my key!"

Well, Gerry went to such a lot of trouble to get the mouse a new key. He went to the toyshop and asked for one, but they said they couldn't take keys out of any of the animals there. So that wasn't any good.

Then he had a good idea and went to the clock-shop – and a little key there fitted the mouse exactly! Wasn't that lucky?

The mouse was so very pleased to be able to run about again that when the monkey wound him up that night he tore round as fast as an express train! The doll's-house dolls gave a little party to show how glad they were, and everyone was happy.

The mouse couldn't say enough about Gerry because he was so happy at having a new key. "He's a wonderful boy," he

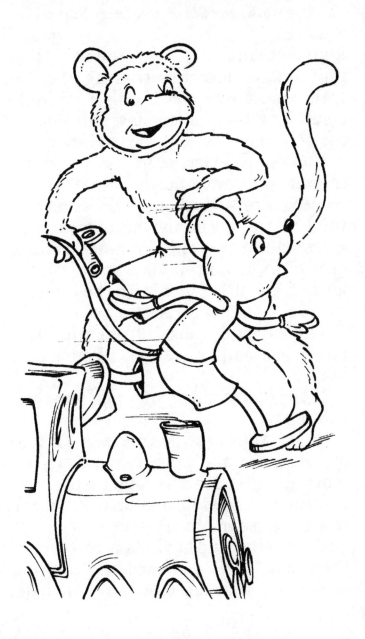

kept saying to everyone. "He's marvellous! Fancy bothering about a little mouse like me! If only I could do something for him one day! But I'm too little to be of any real use to Gerry."

Now one day Gerry came into his room as excited as could be.

"Hello, toys!" he said. "What do you think? I'm going on the bus to my cousin Billy's all by myself! I'm really getting grown up, I can tell you! Look, Mum's given me a little purse with the bus fare in."

The toys all stared up at the little brown leather purse. It had a pound coin in it.

"I've got to change my shoes and then I'm ready."

He put the purse down beside his feet on the floor and began to put on his outdoor shoes. He was soon ready.

"Hurry!" called his mother. "You don't want to miss the bus, Gerry."

Gerry stood up and then ran out of the room. The toys heard him running down the passage to the front door,

shouting goodbye to his mother.

And then the monkey saw that Gerry had left the little brown purse on the floor! He had forgotten it – and inside was the money for the bus. Oh dear – now what was to be done?

"He won't be able to pay for his ticket," said the monkey. "He won't be able to go."

"Poor Gerry," said the teddy bear, sadly.

"What a disappointment," said the clown.

"I'm going after him!" cried the clockwork mouse, in his high, squeaky voice. "Wind me up, Monkey. Tie the purse on to my back, Teddy. Hurry!"

While the monkey was winding him up, the teddy tied the little purse firmly on to the small mouse's back. Then off he rushed out of the door, down the passage, out of the front door, down the path, and into the street!

You should have seen him go! He had never run so fast in his life. He really whirred along. Far in front of him was Gerry. The mouse panted along, hoping

he would catch the boy. Suddenly Gerry stopped and clapped his hand to his pocket. He had suddenly remembered the purse. He had left it behind. He stared in dismay for he could see the bus coming round the corner!

And at that very moment something brushed against his shoe! It was the little mouse! Gerry looked down and stared in astonishment. He saw the purse at once and pulled it off the mouse's back.

"I can't believe it!" he kept saying to himself. "I can't believe it. You can't really have come after me with my purse and yet you have!"

He hadn't time to do anything more than take the purse, for the bus was stopping. He rushed off – and the clockwork mouse watched him get on the bus. The little creature was very happy.

"I've been of some real use to Gerry at last," he said, and ran happily back home.

And on the way home he had an adventure – yes, a real adventure! A cat saw him running by and thought he was

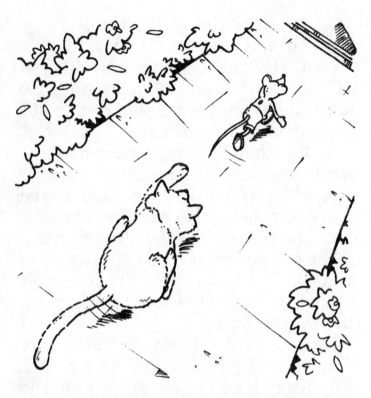

a real mouse. She sprang after him and he tore away as fast as ever he could.

In at the gate he went, down the path and through the front door. And there his clockwork ran down – but the monkey was waiting for him and wound him up again. So he was able to run safely into Gerry's room and stop there, panting and excited, to tell the toys his adventures.

Everyone praised him and made a fuss of him. "You ought to have a medal, or something," said the monkey.

Well, he did have something! Gerry brought home a little red ribbon and tied it round his neck.

"That's to show you are the best clockwork mouse in the world!" he said. And dear me, wasn't the mouse proud! He's still got that ribbon, and he'll tell you why, if you ask him.

The Dog with
the Very Long Tail

There was once a dog with a very long tail. His name was Ginger, because he was just the colour of ginger, and he belonged to little Terry Brown.

Terry was fond of Ginger. He went about everywhere with his dog, and played games with him when he came out of school. Ginger loved Terry too, and would have done anything in the world for him. His tail never stopped wagging when he was with Terry.

One day Terry was very excited. There was to be a grand garden party in the Rectory garden, with sweet-stalls, competitions, baby shows and dog shows. Terry was going, and he made up his mind to buy some peppermint sweets and to have a bottle of ginger beer and two dips in the bran-tub.

"There's to be a maypole dance too," he told his mother, "and I shall watch that. Mr Jones is having a coconut shy, and I shall have two tries at that."

"Well, I will give you a pound to spend," said his mother. "That should be plenty for everything, Terry."

"Oh, thank you," said Terry. "I shall take Ginger with me and buy him a bar of chocolate. He'll love that."

When the day came Terry and Ginger walked to the garden party. Terry had

the one pound coin in his pocket, and he was planning all he would do with it. He looked round the grounds and decided that he would start with a go at the coconut shy. He thought it would be lovely to win a big nut.

"I'll have a go," he said to the man. "How much?"

"Three balls for ten pence," said the man. Terry put his hand into his pocket to get his money – and, oh dear me – it was gone! There was a hole at the bottom and the coin had dropped out!

Terry was so upset. He went back to look for his money but he couldn't find it anywhere. Ginger went with him and was just as upset as his master.

"Now I can't buy any sweets or ginger beer, or have any dips in the bran-tub," said poor Terry, sadly. "All my money is gone. Oh, Ginger, I do think it's bad luck, don't you?"

Ginger pushed his nose into Terry's hand and looked up at him with big brown eyes. He was very sorry for his master. He thought he would go and look for the lost money by himself, so he trotted off, nose to ground, trying to find the coin.

Suddenly Ginger came to where a great many dogs were all gathered together with their masters and mistresses, and he ran up to a collie dog called Rover, a great friend of his.

"What are you all doing here?" he asked Rover.

"Waiting for the dog shows," answered Rover.

"I hope you win a prize," said Ginger.

"Aren't you going in for the show?" asked Rover.

"No," said Ginger, wagging his tail. "My little master, Terry, is very sad. He has just lost all his money and I'm looking for it."

Just at that moment the dog show began, and the dogs moved into the ring. Ginger stayed to watch. It was a comic dog show, and there were prizes for the fattest dog, the thinnest dog, the dog with the saddest eyes, and the dog with the shortest legs. Ginger thought it was very funny.

"Now then!" cried the man who was running the dog show. "Which dog has the longest tail! Come along, everybody! I've got a measuring tape here to measure the tails with! Bring in your dogs! The one with the longest tail gets a pound!"

Now when Ginger heard that, a good idea suddenly came into his head! Surely no dog had a longer tail than his! Everybody laughed at his tail because it was so very long. He would trot into the ring and show it to the judge!

So Ginger pushed his way through the people watching and trotted into the ring, where other dogs stood having their tails measured.

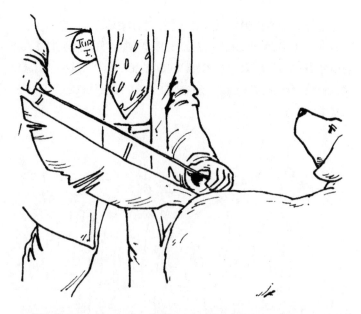

Ginger went right up to the judge and stuck his tail out to be measured.

"Ha!" cried the judge. "Here is a dog who thinks his tail is quite the longest! Stand still, dog, and let me measure it!"

All the people laughed and Ginger stood quite still while the judge measured his tail.

"My goodness, what a long one!" he cried. "Why, it's half a metre long! Little dog, I think you must have the prize! Who is the owner of this dog? Will he please step forward and take the prize?"

Now Terry happened to be peeping at the dog show at that moment and most astonished to see his dog. He was still more surprised to hear that Ginger had won a prize, and he stepped into the ring to take it for him.

"One pound!" said the judge, and he gave a nice bright coin to Terry. Then he patted Ginger and the grateful dog licked his hand.

"Good old Ginger!" said Terry, running off with him. "Fancy you thinking of putting yourself in for the longest-tailed dog! I know why you did it, Ginger! You did it because you were sorry that I had lost my money! You're the cleverest, dearest dog in the world, and I'm going to buy you a bun, two biscuits and a bar of chocolate!"

Ginger wagged his long tail and barked for joy. He bounded along by Terry and when his little master had bought him all that he had said he would, he wagged his long tail quite two hundred times a minute.

"Wuff, wuff!" he said, and he ate up the bun, the biscuits, and the chocolate in one gulp!

"Good old Ginger," said Terry. "Now come along to the coconut shy! I'll see if I can't get a coconut this time!"

Off they went – and Terry knocked down the largest coconut of the lot! Wasn't he lucky? Then he went to buy some sweets and some ginger beer, and had three dips in the bran-tub – all with Ginger's pound; and you may be sure there wasn't a prouder dog than Ginger at the garden party that day!

Pipkin Plays
a Trick

Pipkin and Pinny were very pleased with themselves. They were two pixies who lived in the middle of Chuckle Village. They had just finished making a beautiful gravel path that stretched right from their front door to their gate, quite a long way. It was a nice wide path, made of fine yellow gravel.

"It ought to be watered and rolled now," said Pipkin. "We've shovelled down the gravel, but it's very rough to the feet. If we water it and roll it well, it will be lovely." So they went to get their watering-can and their roller. The watering-can was all right, but alas, their roller was broken! It was no use at all.

"We must borrow one," said Pinny. "Mr Grip has a nice one. Let's go and ask him if he will lend it to us."

So they went to Mr Grip's house – but he was a surly fellow and wouldn't lend them the roller.

"No," he said, "I don't lend things to pixies. They are too careless."

"We're not careless!" said Pipkin, quite cross. "We always look after things that are lent to us and take them back again."

But Mr Grip banged his door in their faces and the two pixies had to go.

"We'll ask Dame Roundy if she'll lend us her roller," said Pinny, hopefully. "Hers is a big one."

So off they went to Dame Roundy's. She was making cakes and said she didn't have time to get the key of her garden shed.

"Go and ask someone else," she said, impatiently. "I can't be bothered about it now."

Pipkin and Pinny went away. They thought it was very unkind of Dame Roundy.

"We'll go to the gnome Chiffle-Chuffle," said Pipkin. "His roller is very big indeed."

They knocked at the door of Chiffle-Chuffle's house. There was no answer. But Pipkin suddenly saw the gnome's face peeping through the window at them, and he called him.

"Chiffle-Chuffle, answer the door! We've come to ask you to lend us your big roller."

The gnome slipped his head inside and made no answer. He was pretending not to be in. He didn't want to lend his roller to the pixies.

Pipkin and Pinny knocked as loudly as they could once more, for they knew quite well that Chiffle-Chuffle was at home – but it was no good, he wouldn't open the door. So off they went down the garden path, very angry with Chiffle-Chuffle for being so mean.

"There's only Mrs Tippitty left who's got a roller," said Pinny. "Oh, I do hope she will lend it to us. She's such a cross old thing that I'm afraid she won't."

He was quite right. Mrs Tippitty was in a very bad temper that afternoon, and when she heard that the pixies wanted to borrow her roller she went quite purple with rage.

"What, lend my splendid roller to two careless pixies like you!" she cried. "Whatever next? No, indeed – and run away quickly before I box your ears!"

You should have seen Pipkin and Pinny run! They knew quite well that Mrs Tippitty meant what she said, for she had often boxed their ears before.

They went home and looked sadly at their gravel path. It did so badly want rolling.

And then Pipkin had a great idea. He whispered it to Pinny, who was simply delighted.

"When Mr Grip, Dame Roundy, Chiffle-Chuffle and Mrs Tippitty come by our cottage today on their way back from their shopping we will play your trick on them," said Pinny. "It's a clever plan!"

What do you think it was? Ah, you wait and see!

After tea Mr Grip, Dame Roundy, Chiffle-Chuffle and Mrs Tippitty all passed by to do their shopping in Chuckle Village. Pipkin and Pinny watched them from their window.

"In about half an hour they'll be back again," said Pipkin, excited. "Go out and hide that penny of yours down deep in the gravel, Pinny."

Pinny slipped out and dug a little hole in the new gravel path. He hid a penny there and then carefully covered it up. Then he and Pipkin waited for the shoppers to return. Chiffle-Chuffle came first, carrying a big bag of potatoes.

As soon as the pixies saw him they pretended to be very busy hunting for something in the gravel path. He stopped to ask them if they had lost something.

"There's some money somewhere in the gravel," said Pipkin.

"I'll help you look for it," said Chiffle-Chuffle, hoping that if he found it the two pixies would give him some of it for his trouble. So in at the gate he came and began to walk up and down the new gravel path looking for the money. He had enormous feet, and how they crunched the gravel as he walked.

Then Dame Roundy, as plump as her name, and with big galoshes on her feet, peeped over the gate, looking in surprise at the two pixies and the gnome hunting up and down the path.

"What are you looking for?" she asked.

"Money," said the gnome Chiffle-Chuffle. "We don't need your help. Go away."

Well, of course, Dame Roundy wasn't going to be ordered away by Chiffle-Chuffle like that! No, she got very red and glared at the gnome in a rage.

"Oh, you want to find the money and keep it for yourself, do you, Chiffle-Chuffle!" she said. "Well, I'll just come in and look too, to see fair play!"

To the pixies' great delight in she came and began to plod up and down the gravel path with her heavy galoshes, looking and looking for the money.

"She's better than a roller!" whispered Pipkin to Pinny. "Her galoshes squash the gravel down beautifully!"

Soon along came Mr Grip and Mrs Tippitty, walking together. They stopped in surprise when they saw so many people walking up and down the pixies' gravel path.

"Come and help too!" cried Dame Roundy. "We are looking for some money!"

In went Mr Grip and Mrs Tippitty, eager to join the fun. Mrs Tippitty had small feet so she really wasn't much use to press down the gravel, but Mr Grip had his great wellington boots on, and they were fine for the gravel.

Well, you should have seen them all hunting up and down that gravel path, looking for the money. They didn't know it was only a penny, they just hunted and hunted. And the gravel path got smoother and smoother and smoother, just as if it had been carefully rolled by their rollers! It was fine to see it, and the two pixies couldn't help chuckling.

At last when the path was as smooth as could be, Pipkin and Pinny thought that it was time for everyone to go.

"Never mind about looking any more," said Pinny. "Thank you all very much. You haven't found the money, but you've made our path nice and smooth for us."

Then Mr Grip, Dame Roundy, Chiffle-Chuffle and Mrs Tippitty all suddenly remembered that the pixies had asked to borrow their rollers that day – and they looked at the path and saw how their feet had flattened it out nicely, almost as well as a roller would have done. Then they knew that a trick had been played on them and they were angry.

"It's a trick!" cried Mrs Tippitty.

"There isn't any money in the path!" roared Chiffle-Chuffle.

"It's because we wouldn't lend the pixies our rollers!" shouted Mr Grip.

"I'll smack them!" said Dame Roundy. But the pixies were too quick for her. They ran into their house and banged the door. Pipkin opened the window and leaned out.

"There is some money in the gravel!" he cried. "There really is."

"Well, you tell us where it is, or we'll punish you," said Mr Grip, shaking his fist.

"Yes, and we'll keep the money too, for our trouble in looking for it!" cried Dame Roundy.

"Well, if we tell you where it is and let you share it between you, will you go away quietly and not worry us any more?" said Pinny.

"Yes!" shouted everyone.

"Do you see that red snapdragon leaning over the path just there?" said Pinny. "Well, dig up the path a little by it and you'll find the money."

Mr Grip did as Pinny said; and very soon found the penny. He picked it up and looked at it. When he saw it was only a penny he was so angry that he flung it straight at the two grinning pixies, who had their heads out of the window to see what was happening.

The others, who hadn't seen that it was only a penny were angry with Mr Grip for throwing the money to Pipkin and Pinny. They ran at him and if he hadn't slipped out of the gate very quickly indeed he would have had his coat pulled right off! He tore down the lane and Dame Roundy, Chiffle-Chuffle and Mrs Tippitty raced after him.

Pipkin and Pinny watched them all running down the road and laughed till they cried. Then they picked up the

penny and put it into their money-box.

"That will teach Dame Roundy and the others not to be so mean about lending things another time," said Pinny, looking at his nice smooth gravel path.

"Yes, it will," said Pipkin, rubbing his hands together in delight. "They've wasted lots of time in looking for a penny which they didn't get in the end – and they've flattened out our new path for us nicely! Ha, ha, ho, ho!"

You should see the path. It's the best in Chuckle Village!

Muddy-One and Pranky

"There goes old Muddy-One!" said the big water snail. "Look out, you young frogs."

The little frogs swam up to the top of the pond at once. They were all afraid of Muddy-One. He was a large, ugly grub who lurked in the mud and was always hungry.

Curly-Shell, the snail, wasn't at all afraid of Muddy-One. He had only to curl himself up in his hard shell whenever he spied the big grub, and nobody could harm him then. But most of the other creatures in the pond were afraid of the ugly old grub.

Pranky, the water pixie, teased him dreadfully. He was a naughty little mischief, very quick and cheeky, and the names he called Muddy-One made all the snails and fishes laugh.

Muddy-One had been in the pond for a very long time. He had been small at first, but now he was big. He crawled about in the mud, and across his face he put a curious claw, which could shoot out and catch any little water creature in its pincers.

He didn't like being teased by Pranky. "I can't help being ugly," he would say. "I didn't make myself. If I could have made myself I would have given myself beautiful wings, and a gleaming body, and I wouldn't live down here in the slimy mud, but up in the sunshine. Sometimes I crawl up a water plant and look out of the water. Up there is a lovely world of light and warmth. I wish I belonged to it."

"Well, you don't! An ugly creature like you wouldn't be allowed to live up in the bright sunshine," said Pranky, and he poked the grub with a bit of stick. "How lazy you are! Stir yourself! Gallop round the pond a bit."

But Muddy-One wasn't very gallopy. He didn't like being poked with a stick, and he was angry with the unkind little pixie. But that only made Pranky call him ruder names than ever; so in the end Muddy-One buried himself deep down in the slime and tried to hide.

"He's ashamed of himself, and I don't wonder," cried Pranky, poking his stick into the mud. "What a pity somebody doesn't eat him. I'll find a big fish one day, Muddy-One, and send him along to eat you."

"You shouldn't tease Muddy-One so," said the big water snail. "He doesn't do you any harm. You're unkind."

Then Pranky swam to the snail and tried to pull him out of his shell. But he couldn't. So he wrote a rude sentence on the snail's shell and left him. He put "I am a poor old slowcoach" all over the snail's shell, and the snail couldn't think why everyone who met him laughed.

Pranky was just as much at home in the air as in the water. He was lucky, for he could run and swim and fly. He was a fine-looking pixie too, and he knew it. He often used a shining dewdrop as a mirror, and looked at himself proudly in it.

One day the Princess Melisande thought she would give a party. Now, she lived high up on a hill above the clouds, so it was plain that every guest would have to fly there.

"I shall get my peacock butterfly to take me," said Jinky the fairy.

"I'm going on Zoom the bumble-bee," said Tippy the goblin.

"I've got my lovely tiger moth," said Twink the elf.

"What are you going on, Pranky?" asked Jinky.

"I shall ask the bluebottle to fly to Princess Melisande's with me," said Pranky. "He's such a lovely colour."

But he couldn't ride the bluebottle because somebody saw it crawling with dirty feet over a baby's bottle, and the baby's mother chased it far away.

"He's a dirty, horrid bluebottle fly," said the mother. "He'll make the baby ill."

So there was no bluebottle for the pixie to ride on. He was upset. "Can I ride on Zoom with you?" he asked Tippy.

"No. He says you once sewed up the end of a foxglove flower when he had crawled inside, and he couldn't get out," said Tippy. "He doesn't like you."

"Well, can I come on your butterfly?" Pranky asked Jinky.

"No, you can't. He isn't strong enough to carry two of us," said Jinky. "Why don't you get a dragonfly? He'd be very strong indeed, and very beautiful too. He would fly so fast that you'd be at the Princess's in no time!"

"Oooh, yes! – I'd love a dragonfly," said Pranky, thinking how very grand he would feel riding such a lovely creature. "But I haven't seen any yet. Where can I get one?"

"You'd better go and ask old Mother Wimple," said Jinky. "She knows all the insects well. She's always mending their wings for them when they get torn. She could get you a dragonfly, I expect. But be polite to her, Pranky, because she's got a hot temper."

Pranky flew off. He soon came to where Mother Wimple lived. She had a tiny house by the pond, and she was sitting outside it, busily patching the torn wing of a butterfly.

"Mother Wimple, I'm going to Princess Melisande's party," said Pranky, sitting down beside her. "And her palace is so high above the clouds that I've got to get an insect to take me. I would like a dragonfly. Could you get me one, please?"

"You're very polite all of a sudden," said old Mother Wimple, who had not heard very good tales of Pranky. "You're one of those people who have very good manners when they want something, and can be very rude when they don't, aren't you?"

"Oh, no!" said Pranky, going rather red. "No, I'm very well behaved, Mother Wimple. Please do tell me if you can get me a dragonfly."

"When is the party?" asked Mother Wimple.

"Tomorrow afternoon," said Pranky.

"Come back an hour before you have to set off for the party, and I'll have here the finest dragonfly you ever saw," said Mother Wimple.

Pranky flew off in delight. He was back in good time the next day, but he couldn't

see any dragonfly.

"Be patient," said Mother Wimple. "You'll see him soon. Ah – here he comes."

She pointed to a water plant whose stem came right up out of the pond. Up it was crawling the ugly old grub, Muddy-One. Pranky stared at him and then he stared at Mother Wimple.

"Why – that's no dragonfly. That's only ugly old Muddy-One!" he said.

"Oh, you know him, do you?" said Mother Wimple. "Well now, you watch and see what is going to happen to him. You'll see something marvellous."

Pranky watched. Old Muddy-One crawled right out of the water, and clung to the stem of the water plant, enjoying the hot sunshine.

Then, to the pixie's enormous surprise, the ugly old grub split his skin right down his back!

"Gracious goodness, look at that!" said Pranky. "He's split himself. Has he eaten too much? I always told him he'd burst if he was so greedy."

"Be quiet," said Mother Wimple. "Now look – he's split even further."

Pranky watched in surprise. He saw that the ugly old grub was trying to creep out of his own skin. How extraordinary!

But what a different creature came out of the old skin! He had a long, slender body that gleamed blue green. He had crumpled wings. He had enormous eyes that shone in the sun, and six weak legs that clung to the water plant for safety.

"Why – Muddy-One's got wings," cried Pranky. "Look – he's spreading them out in the sun to dry them. They are long and lovely, and look at his beautiful blue-green body and eyes. Oh, Mother Wimple, he's not an ugly water grub any longer, he's a most beautiful dragonfly. It's magic, it's magic! Oh, how clever of you to make a dragonfly come out of Muddy's old skin."

"I didn't," said Mother Wimple. "All dragonflies live down in the mud as grubs for a long time. But when the right time comes, they creep up into the sunshine, take off their old skin, and dart up into the air – bright, beautiful dragonflies!"

"Oh, I shall love to ride him," cried Pranky. Mother Wimple called to the dragonfly as he sat sunning his wings.

"Swift-One! Come here and take this pixie to Princess Melisande's party."

The dragonfly flew over to Mother Wimple and soared round her head, gleaming in the sun.

Pranky stood up in delight. "Let me ride you, let me ride you!" he cried.

Swift-One the dragonfly flew just out of reach. "What! Let you, a rude and ill-mannered pixie, ride me, the swiftest dragonfly in the world? Certainly not! I haven't forgotten how you teased me and the names you called me, you horrid little pixie!"

"That's not the way to talk, Swift-One," said Mother Wimple sternly. "I have promised Pranky that he shall ride you. Come down, so that he may get on your back."

Swift-One darted down, and Pranky leaped on to his back. The dragonfly soared high in the air at such a pace that Pranky's breath was almost taken away. But then Swift-One began to play tricks.

He stopped suddenly in mid-air, and Pranky almost shot over his head. He flew upside-down, and Pranky nearly fell off. He darted down to the surface of the pond and made the pixie get his feet wet. He teased Pranky just as much as Pranky had once teased him, down in

99

the pond. Then he turned over and over and over in the air, and at last, the pixie, too giddy to hold on any longer, fell off and flew down to the ground, landing beside Mother Wimple with a bump.

He began to cry when he saw the dragonfly darting away at top speed. Mother Wimple laughed.

"It serves you right," she said. "I thought he would play a few tricks on you if he had the chance. Cry, Pranky, cry! Perhaps you will learn now not to make fun of ugly, slow creatures. You never know when they are going to change into beautiful, swift flying things that will tip you off their backs."

"I c-c-c-can't go to the party now," wept Pranky. "Tippy's gone by on his butterfly, and Jinky's gone on Zoom the bumble-bee, but I've got no one to take me!"

He went home, very sorry for himself. And all that August and September he had to keep a sharp look out for Swift-One, because the dragonfly flew down to tease the bad little pixie whenever he saw him.

Have you seen Swift-One, the dragonfly? Look out for him. He's beautiful.

Biddy's
Toys

Biddy was playing in the garden with her teddy bear when her mother called her indoors in a hurry. "It's time to get changed to go to Auntie's," she said. "Hurry, dear!"

Biddy ran indoors at once, and she quite forgot to take her teddy with her. He was left lying on the grass and he didn't like it a bit.

It poured with rain that evening and the teddy got drenched through. He began to sneeze, and two brownies who were hurrying by heard him.

"You poor thing!" they said. "You'll get such a cold out here in the damp. You'd better come with us into our tree. It's nice and warm there."

So they took him to their home in the

old oak-tree, and put him in front of the little oil-stove they had there. He began to dry and stopped sneezing.

Now Biddy was in bed and asleep by this time – but she suddenly woke up and remembered her teddy bear.

"I left him out in the garden! Poor, poor teddy!" she said. "It's been raining and he'll be so wet and cold. I shall fetch him."

She was a sensible little girl and knew that she would catch cold too if she went into the wet night with nothing on but her nightie. So she put on her rubber boots, a woollen jumper, her dressing-gown and a mackintosh. Wasn't she sensible? Then out she went.

Well, of course, her teddy wasn't there! She hunted here and hunted there, but she couldn't find him. The two brownies heard someone near their tree and they slipped out to see who it was.

"It's the little girl who left her poor teddy out," they whispered. "Let's catch her and take her before the brownie king. He will punish her for being unkind to her toys."

So before Biddy knew what was happening, she felt her arms being held behind her, and she was marched off through the night by the two brownies!

"Let me go!" she cried. "You've no right to take me away like this!"

"We're taking you before the brownie king to tell him that you ill-treat your toys," one of the brownies said sternly.

"I don't!" cried Biddy.

"Yes, you do," said the brownies, and marched her up to a little doorway that had a yellow lamp burning above it. They knocked seven times and the door opened. Another brownie led them into a big room where sat the brownie king on a gold and silver throne.

"Please, Your Majesty, we've brought before you a little girl who is unkind to her toys," said the two brownies.

"Dear, dear, I'm getting quite tired of seeing these naughty children and punishing them," said the king impatiently. "What a lot of boys and girls there are who don't know how to treat their toys!"

"I am very kind to my toys," said Biddy, indignantly. "It's horrid of you to say these things about me!"

"Well, these brownies wouldn't have brought you here if they hadn't had a

good reason," said the king. "What did you bring her for, brownies?"

"Please, Your Majesty, this girl left her teddy bear out on the grass, and it poured with rain. He got wet through, and now has a very bad, sneezing cold," said the brownies, both together. The king frowned.

"I know I left him out," said Biddy. "But it's the very first time I ever did, and I didn't mean to. When I woke up in the middle of the night, I remembered him, poor thing, and got out of bed to go and find him. That shows how much I care for my teddy, doesn't it?"

"Well, it doesn't sound as if you were really an unkind little girl," said the king. "Have you anyone who can speak for you?"

"Only my toys," said Biddy. "If they could speak they would tell you I am as kind to them as I can be."

"Fetch this girl's toys here," said the king, and to Biddy's great surprise a brownie ran off to fetch her dolls and toys. In about ten minutes, in they all came! How astonished Biddy was to see her dolls walking in, to see her donkey and blue rabbit come in side by side, and her elephant solemnly carrying on his back her little toy soldiers! They all stared at the king, and then they saw Biddy. With cries of joy they ran to her, chattering eagerly, but the brownies waved them back in a row against the wall.

"Toys," said the king, "this girl, your little mistress, has been brought before me because, so these two brownies say, she is unkind to you. What have you to say about it?"

The biggest doll stepped out.

"Your Majesty," she said, "Biddy is a very kind little girl. Why, when I broke my arm, she took me to the dolls' hospital and I got a new one!"

Then the baby doll stepped out.

"Your Majesty," she said, in her babyish voice, "I love Biddy. She always puts me to bed every night and takes the greatest care of me."

Then the sailor doll stepped out.

"Your Majesty," he said, "Biddy is a darling. I am a sailor doll, but I hadn't a ship – and do you know, Biddy spent her pocket money on a boat for me. Wasn't that kind?"

Everybody clapped at this, and the sailor doll smiled all over his red face. Then the donkey moved forward.

"Your Majesty," he cried, "it's all nonsense about Biddy being unkind to us. Look at my black mane! When it got thin Biddy made me a whole new mane out of some black wool, which I'm wearing now. What do you think of that for kindness?"

The blue rabbit ran out and stood beside the donkey. "Please, Your Majesty," he said in a squeaky voice, "I must say a word for Biddy too. One day I got a hole in my blue skin and all my sawdust began to come out – but Biddy saw it and carefully sewed me up again. She's very, very kind!"

Everybody cheered again, and then the elephant lumbered forward with all the soldiers on his back.

"Biddy rides on me," he said, "but she never lets more than one person ride on me at once, in case I break. Now, Your Majesty, plenty of children ride their toys till they break in pieces – so I think Biddy is a dear!"

"So do we, so do we!" shouted all the toy soldiers. "Look at us! We haven't a single broken arm or leg among us, which shows how carefully Biddy puts us away each night in our box. She doesn't leave us out on the floor to be trampled on, as many children do to their soldiers!"

"Well, well, well," said the brownie king, in surprise. "What a very unusual, kindly, goodhearted little girl this Biddy is. Where's the teddy bear that was left out in the rain?"

At that very moment he walked in. He had heard that Biddy was being judged for unkindness by the brownie king, and he had hurried to save her.

"Your Majesty," he cried, "listen to me! It was quite an accident that Biddy left me out in the rain. And when she remembered, didn't she come out all by herself in the dark, cold night, to find me? I tell you, she's a darling, and I love her."

He ran to Biddy and hugged her leg, for he was too small to reach anything else. All the other toys ran to her too, and Biddy was so pleased that she nearly cried.

"Biddy is free to go home," said the king. "She is kind, not unkind, and it was not right to bring her here. Brownies, say you're sorry!"

The two brownies came over to Biddy and said they were sorry. They looked very red and ashamed of themselves, so Biddy said it was quite all right, she really didn't mind.

"Anyhow, it is lovely to see how my toys love me," she said. "Come on, my dears, we'll all go home together, and get to bed. We shall be so sleepy in the morning!"

So home they all went together, as happy as could be. I wonder if your toys love you as much as Biddy's love her. I hope they do, don't you?

The Three
Bad Boys

"I say!" said Harry. "Did you know the early plums are ripe in Mr Jones's orchard?"

"No. Are they?" said Jack. "I vote we go and get some of them!"

"Rather!" said Ben. "When shall we go? Is old Mr Jones ever about? He's a real crosspatch and I wouldn't want to be caught by him!"

"He's gone to help his brother run the greengrocer's shop down in the town," said Harry. "It would be quite safe to go this evening, I should think. They don't shut the shop till half past five and after that they always clear up."

"Right – meet at the orchard gate at five," said Jack. "We'll have plenty of time to slip into the field, climb the plum-

114

trees, and pick what we want before Mr Jones comes home."

"Oooh – lovely ripe plums!" said Ben. "I shall fill my pockets full."

The three boys met outside the orchard gate. Mr Jones's cottage looked empty and locked up. No one was about. It was a lonely place and nobody was likely to come by.

"Come on – over the gate we go," said Ben, and over they went.

The orchard wasn't very big and had hedges all round it. The boys made their way to where the early plums hung purple and ripe on the trees. What beauties! And then there came a movement behind some bushes at one end of the orchard. The boys stopped. Something trotted round the bush and stood there, looking at the boys.

"Pooh – only a goat," said Harry. "Come on." Another goat appeared, and another and another. They stood looking at the boys. And then the first one made a run at them. He put his head down to butt them.

"Run, quick!" yelled Ben. They made for the trees and shinned up them just in time. The four goats gathered round the trees, looking up. One goat made a loud bleating noise.

"I hope he's not calling Mr Jones," said Ben, nervously. "Be quiet, you silly goat!"

"And go away," ordered Harry, feeling much braver now he was up the tree. The goats didn't go away. They wandered

round the plum trees, looking up at the three boys.

"I say," said Jack, after a time, "I just heard the church clock striking half past five. Mr Jones will be home soon. I wish these goats would go away, back to the bushes."

In about five minutes the goats began to wander off. The boys slithered down the trees at once. They felt rather full up because they had each spent their time eating a few pounds of plums!

"Now – run for it," said Ben, and they ran.

But the goats ran, too, of course! *Bump – thud – biff!* They charged at the backs of the three boys, and over they all went!

"Ooooh! Ow! OOOH!" yelled the boys, trying to escape. Harry managed to get to the gate and leap on it. Ben was butted all round the field before he managed to escape and poor Jack scrambled through a prickly hedge and tore a big hole in his blazer!

They raced down the lane and bumped into Mr Jones round the corner. Some

plums fell out of Harry's pocket and rolled over the road.

"Hey, you! You've been stealing my plums, you bad boys!" cried Mr Jones. "Stop!" But they didn't stop.

They raced away and disappeared. Oh, how bruised they were! They simply couldn't sit down that evening.

They were very ill that night because some of the plums they had eaten had not been ripe. But they had to go to school in the morning just the same, because their mothers were so cross with them for coming home dirty and with their clothes torn.

And at school there was a message to the headmaster from Mr Jones, complaining that three boys had stolen his plums.

"Now, which of you was it?" said the headmaster, sternly, eyeing the boys standing in rows before him. "Own up,

please. I warn you that I shall know, even if you don't tell me."

Ben, Harry, and Jack said nothing. They knew that Mr Jones hadn't known any of them. So how could the head know?

"Sit," said the headmaster suddenly, and the boys sat down on their hard forms. The head watched them all.

"Ben, Harry, and Jack, come up here," he said. "You are the thieves. You will each pay Mr Jones for the plums you have stolen."

"B-b-but sir – how do you know it was us?" stammered Ben, surprised.

"Because Mr Jones said that he kept goats in his orchard to butt bad boys who went there to steal," said the head, grimly. "And when I said to you all, 'Sit,' I watched to see which of you had to sit down very, very carefully. That's how I knew it was you, Ben, and you, Jack, and you, Harry! Well, I hope you think the plums were worth it!"

"No, sir, they weren't," said Harry. "We were dreadfully butted – we were ill in the night – and now we have to pay Mr Jones for plums we could have bought from his shop anyway. Please don't laugh, sir – it's not funny!"

But everyone thought it was very funny, and the whole school roared every time they saw the three bad boys trying to sit down comfortably.

Poor Harry, Jack, and Ben – they don't feel as if they can ever eat a plum again!

The Wizard's Pink Cloak

Hey-Presto the wizard had a wonderful cloak. Whenever he swung it round his shoulders he disappeared at once, because it had very powerful magic in it.

The cloak was most useful to the wizard. He wore it whenever he wanted to be invisible, and then he was able to do all kinds of things.

He could slip into other wizards' castles and watch them at their magic work without being seen. He could go into witch Green-Eyes' cottage and stand unseen beside her as she stirred spells into her big black pot. He could swing his cloak round him when visitors came that he didn't want to bother about. Nobody could see him then!

"A most useful cloak!" said Hey-

Presto, whenever he hung it up in his cupboard and locked the door. "An invaluable cloak! I couldn't do without it. I must never, never let my enemies get it."

One day when he took it out of the cupboard, Miggy, his old servant, saw it.

"Good gracious, Master!" she said. "How can you wear that dirty old cloak? What colour is it meant to be? It's so dirty that I can't even tell if it's blue, red or green!"

"It's pink," said the wizard, looking at it. "At least, it's supposed to be pink! It does look dirty, doesn't it? Well, well – I suppose I've used it for over a hundred years now – no wonder it is dirty!"

"It's smelly, too," said Miggy, wrinkling her nose. "Pooh! It needs washing, Master. Fancy using a thing for over a hundred years and not having it washed. And look at this hole!"

"Dear me, yes," said the wizard, quite alarmed. "It won't do to get big holes in it – bits of me will be seen then, through the holes. Whatever shall I do?"

"I'll wash and mend it," said Miggy, firmly.

"It's too precious," said Hey-Presto, clutching it tightly.

"Now listen," said Miggy. "That cloak smells so dirty that very soon people will know you are near them, even though you're invisible. You let me wash it. I'll be very, very careful."

"All right, Miggy. But when you hang it out to dry, please put up a clothes-line in the walled garden and make sure the gate is locked," said Hey-Presto. "If anyone saw this cloak on the line they might steal it!"

"Oh, Master, I'll be as careful of your cloak as if it were made of gold!" said old Miggy, putting it over her arm. "My word – what a horrible smell! It must be five hundred years old, not one!"

She went off and got a tub full of boiling water. In went the magic cloak, and Miggy scrubbed it up and down in the suds.

"Just look at the dirt coming out," said Miggy, in disgust. "Why, there's more dirt than cloak! I'll have to wash it three or four times before it's really clean."

When she had finished washing it, she could hardly believe her eyes! The cloak was pink – the loveliest pink imaginable!

Miggy shook it out and then called her master. "Master, come here! Did you ever see such a lovely colour in your life?"

Hey-Presto looked at his cloak. Why, it didn't seem the same one! "It's the colour of almond blossom!" he said. "It's the colour of wild roses in the hedge! And yes – it's exactly the colour of the sky when it's pink at sunset time!"

"Yes," said Miggy. "Shame on you for wearing it so dirty! I'm going to hang it out to dry and then I'll mend it for you."

"In the walled garden, mind!" called the wizard, anxiously. "Nobody can get in there, nobody at all."

Miggy hurried into the walled garden. She had already put up a washing-line there. She went to the door in the wall and locked it carefully, putting the key into her pocket. Now nobody could get into the garden from outside, and the walls were far too high to climb.

She looked at the clouds racing across the sky. "Nice windy day – the cloak will dry quickly!" she thought. "I'll press it tonight and mend it – and I'll see that the master doesn't get it so dirty again. It shan't go for more than twenty years this time before it's washed again."

She pegged the cloak carefully on the line and watched it flapping in the wind. It would soon be dry!

"I'll fetch it about three o'clock," she thought and trotted indoors. She kept an eye on it through the kitchen window, and was pleased to see that it was drying nicely.

At three o'clock she went into the garden to unpeg the cloak – but it wasn't there! The line was empty – and three or four clothes pegs lay scattered on the ground!

Miggy gave a scream that brought Hey-Presto out at once. "Master! *Master!* Your cloak's been stolen!"

Hey-Presto came at top speed. He saw the empty washing-line and the scattered pegs and he groaned. He ran to the garden door that led out into the lane, but it was locked. No one could have got in that way.

"I kept that cloak under my eye the whole time," sobbed Miggy. "I looked out from the kitchen window almost every minute. Nobody could have got in without my seeing them, nobody! They couldn't get out without being seen either."

"Oh, yes they could," said Hey-Presto, grimly. "All the thief had to do was to swing the cloak round his shoulders and he and the cloak too would be invisible at once. He could go where he liked then – even creep in past you through the kitchen, out into the hall and walk out of the front door. Nobody would see him. What am I to do? My wonderful cloak! I must get it back!"

"The thief won't always be wearing it, sir, and it's such a bright, glowing pink that it would be very easy to recognise it," said poor Miggy, very upset indeed. "Can't you offer a reward, Master, to anyone – even to any animal or bird – who finds it or brings news of it?"

"Yes. Yes, I'll certainly do that," said Hey-Presto. Immediately he sent out hundreds of little pixie heralds, complete with trumpets, to announce his loss and the reward for finding the cloak.

Everyone was excited. The country was searched from top to bottom. But

no news came in. Nobody had ever seen the cloak, hardly anyone had even known of it – so how could it have been stolen?

Rabbits searched down burrows. Fish in the rivers hunted here and there. Owls looked in hollow trees, swallows looked in barns. It was no good – nobody saw anything pink that was big enough to be the cloak.

And then one day a chaffinch flew down to Miggy in great excitement. "Pink!" he called loudly. "Pink-pink!"

"What do you mean? Have you found the pink cloak?" cried Miggy. "Where is it?"

"Pink-pink-pink!" shouted the little chaffinch, fluffing out his pretty chest. "*Pink!*"

"I'll come with you," said Miggy, putting on her bonnet. "Lead the way, Chaffinch. I'm sure you think you've found the cloak!"

"Chip-chip-chip-chip, cherry-erry-erry, chippy, here-we-are!" sang the chaffinch, flying up into a tall tree just outside the walled garden. And there, caught on a high branch, and wrapped round and round it, was the magic cloak, as pink as ever, but a little dirty.

"Yes! You're right! It is the cloak!" cried Miggy. "You clever bird, you very clever

bird! Wait here till I get a ladder, and don't you dare to tell anyone else!"

She fetched a long ladder and up and up she went. She unwrapped the cloak from the branch and slipped it round her so that she might use both her hands to climb down the ladder again. At once, to the chaffinch's astonishment, she vanished and the cloak vanished, too!

"Pink!" he called anxiously. Miggy's voice answered him from the ladder.

"It's all right. I'm still here, climbing down the ladder. Wearing the cloak is the easiest way for me to carry it!"

She ran to the wizard, taking the cloak off just as she got to him. "Master! It's found! Here it is!"

"Where was it?" asked Hey-Presto, startled and delighted.

"Caught up in a tree not far from the walled garden!" said Miggy. "Nobody stole it! The strong wind must have blown it off the line straight up into the tree and wrapped it round a branch – and there it's been ever since!"

"But who found it?" asked Hey-Presto, looking to see if the cloak was damaged.

"The chaffinch who nests in that tree," said Miggy. "He came and told me. He was so excited he could only say, 'Pink! Pink!' But I guessed what he meant, of course."

"Then he must have the reward," said Hey-Presto. "Call him here, the clever bird."

The chaffinch came. He flew in at the window, calling, "Pink! Pink!"

"There! He can't say anything but that

at the moment," said Miggy. "He's been shouting out the news to everyone – he's so proud of himself!"

"Chaffinch, you have earned the reward," said Hey-Presto, and the little bird flew on to his shoulder. "You may have a sack of gold – a box of spells – or anything else you can think of."

The chaffinch whispered a little song into the wizard's ear. Hey-Presto laughed.

"What does he want for a reward?" asked Miggy.

"Nothing! He says money is no use to him – and he's frightened of spells – and as he has a nest of his own, with a dear little wife and four beautiful nestlings, he has got everything he can possibly want," said the wizard. "He just wants to know if he can go on telling everyone that he found my pink cloak – he's so very, very proud of that."

"Well, let him," said Miggy. "It's a reward that won't cost you a penny – and he'll be glad that he and all his family can boast about finding your magic cloak. People love boasting – even birds do!"

"You're right," said Hey-Presto, and he turned to the excited little chaffinch. He spoke very solemnly.

"As your reward for finding my pink cloak you may tell everyone in the world!" he said. "You may shout the news at the top of your voice year after year!"

And, believe it or not, from that day to this every chaffinch shouts out the news each spring and summer. You must listen, you really must.

"Pink!" he calls loudly. "Pink, pink, pink!"

Listen for him, will you, and call out, "Clever bird! Who found the magic cloak? What colour was it?"

And he will put his knowing little head on one side and answer you at once.

"Pink! Pink-pink-pink!"

The Six Little Motor-Cars

Henry had six little motor-cars, all different. One was a car, one was a lorry, one was a milk-van, one was a bus, one was a racer and the last was a builder's van.

They were very old, quite four years old. But they all had their wheels, and they all ran well along the floor. It was only their paint that had gone.

The car had once been blue, and the lorry had been brown. The milk-van had been bright yellow, and the bus red. The racer had been green and the builder's van a brilliant orange. Now all the little cars were grey, without a single bit of their bright colours left.

But Henry still played with them, and loved them. He got them out every week and ran them over the floor, hooting loudly as if he were the six cars. He put them away carefully and didn't tread on them at all.

"How you do love your little cars, Henry," said his mother. "They are getting very old. But you must keep them carefully because I haven't any money to buy you nice little cars like that again for a long time."

Now one day Thomas and his mother came to tea. He was younger than Henry, and he loved cars even more than Henry

did. He had one of his own, quite a big one – but he had no little ones at all. So, when he saw Henry's cars in the toy-cupboard he gave a squeal of delight.

"Oh! Look at those cars! Can we play with them?"

It was nice to have someone else playing at cars, hooting and running them forward and back. The two boys built streets with their bricks and put up posts for traffic-lights. It really was great fun.

And then, when Thomas had to go home, he wanted to take the cars with him! His mother shook her head and said no, he couldn't.

"They belong to Henry," she said. "You have played with them all afternoon. Now you must leave them."

Thomas began to scream. Henry looked at him in disgust. Fancy a boy behaving like that! Why, only babies yelled.

"Oh dear!" said Thomas's mother. "Don't scream, Thomas. You know, Mrs Hill, he has been very unwell, and I have

140

had to give him his own way a lot. The doctor says it is very bad for him to scream. Now do be sensible, Thomas."

But Thomas was not going to be sensible. He screamed till he was purple in the face.

"Henry," said Henry's mother, "will you lend Thomas your cars just for tonight? You can have them back again tomorrow."

Thomas stopped screaming to hear what Henry would say.

"No," said Henry firmly. "I've never

lent my cars to anyone. They are too precious."

"Henry, don't be selfish," said his mother. "Do it to please me. Poor Thomas is so unhappy."

Henry looked at his mother. "Well, Mummy," he said, "I'll lend him them because I want to please you, not because Thomas is unhappy. I think he's naughty, and I don't want him to come to tea again."

Thomas stopped screaming. He looked rather ashamed, but he let his mother put the six cars into his pockets. Henry was sad. He felt sure they would come back broken, with some of the wheels missing. He was sad all that evening. His mother was sorry.

"Henry, I'm glad to have such a kind little boy," she said, when she put him to bed. "You make me very happy."

Well, Henry was glad about that, but he hadn't made himself happy at all! He thought about his precious cars a great deal, and wondered if Thomas was taking care of them.

Next morning Thomas arrived at the front door, with his father this time, not his mother. In his hand he carried a big box. Henry wondered if all his cars were in it.

Thomas came upstairs with his father and the box. "Now, Thomas, what have you got to say to Henry?" said his father.

"Henry, here are your cars," said Thomas, talking as if he were ashamed of himself. "I'm sorry I screamed for them. Daddy was very angry when he knew."

"It's all right," said Henry, taking the box. He didn't like to open it in case he found some of the cars were broken.

"Do open the box," said Thomas. So Henry did open it – and how he stared! Every single one of those little cars had been given a fresh coat of bright paint! There they were in the box, red, orange, blue, green, brown and yellow! They looked marvellous.

"I did that in return for your kindness," said Thomas's father. "And you will find a nice traffic-light indicator there too. Thomas took money from his

money-box and bought it. He's rather ashamed of himself, you see. I'm not surprised you don't want him to come to tea again with you."

"Oh, but I do!" cried Henry, quite changing his mind. "I do! We had a lovely time yesterday with the cars. Oh, aren't they fine now! As good as new. Better! And look at this lovely traffic-light. You can really change the colours."

Thomas came to tea with Henry the next week and the two of them played the whole afternoon with the cars, streets made of bricks and the traffic-light. And when it was time for Thomas to go home again, did he yell and scream for the cars? Not he!

He went home with his mother, sad to leave the cars, but making up his mind never to behave like a baby again.

Henry's mother watched him putting away the little cars.

"It's a funny thing, Henry," she said, "but whenever anyone does something to please somebody else, it always comes back to them. You pleased me – and now Thomas and his father have pleased you! I didn't reward you – but they did!"

It's a pity everyone doesn't know that, isn't it? Kindness always comes back somehow.

The
Quiet Kite

When the kite came to live in the playroom the other toys couldn't understand it at all.

"It's not a doll," said the red-haired doll.

"It's not a bear," said the teddy.

"It's not an engine," said the train.

"It's a silly sort of toy," said the rocking-horse, looking into the toy cupboard, where the kite lay quiet and still. "It has no legs, so it can't run about with us. It can't even roll, like the balls!"

"It has a tail, but doesn't wag it," said the pink dog, who was very proud of his tail because it wagged to and fro when he was wound up.

Everyone looked at the kite's long tail. It was made of lots of screwed-up pieces of paper tied to a long string.

The kite suddenly spoke, in a kind if windy, wheezy voice. "I daren't move my tail in case it gets tangled up," it said. "It takes such a long time to untangle it, you know."

"Oh, the kite can talk!" cried the red-haired doll. "Do come out and play with us, Kite!"

"No, thank you," said the kite. "As the rocking-horse said, I have no legs, so I

can't walk. I prefer to stay here quietly."

And there the kite stayed, and wouldn't move. The toys laughed at it. They pulled its tail. They unwound its string and got it all muddled. The kite was very upset.

"Don't do that," it said. "I may want that string some day."

"Pooh! What for?" cried the teddy bear. "What do kites do? Nothing, so far as I can see! Except just lie about in the cupboard and get lazier and lazier."

And the bad bear tangled the string up even more. The kite was very unhappy about it, for it had no arms or legs to undo the knots.

But the little white ostrich out of the Noah's ark was very kind. She came up to undo the tangle. And very soon the kite and the ostrich made friends.

"Where's the other ostrich?" asked the kite. "I thought there were two of every animal and bird in the ark."

"Well, there were two ostriches," said the little white ostrich, "but the other one got trodden on and broken. So now

there is only me. And I am often lonely because I am by myself. The other animals are in pairs."

"Don't be lonely," said the kite. "Come and talk to me when you feel sad."

So after that the ostrich and the kite often talked together though everyone else laughed at them.

"What you can see in that silly, quiet kite I really can't imagine!" said the teddy bear to the ostrich.

"And what the kite can see in that stupid little wooden ostrich puzzles me!" said the red-haired doll, tossing her head.

Now one day the wind got up out-of-doors and roared away into the sky, blowing the clouds along and twisting the chimney smoke like ribbon. And into the room ran John, to whom all the toys belonged.

"Where's my kite? Where's my kite?" he cried. "It's just the day for a kite! Kite, kite, where are you?"

He pulled the kite out of the cupboard and shook out its tail. "Come along!" he cried. "It's just the day for a fine kite like you!"

His sister Annie came into the room too. "Oh, have you found your kite?" she said. "Good, John. I'll bring all the toys into the garden to watch!"

So she picked up the toys, little white ostrich and all, and followed her brother into the garden. The toys were most surprised. What was all this fuss about the kite? Why was this windy day just the day for it? They simply couldn't imagine!

Annie set the toys down on the grass. John began to unwind a little of the

string that was tied to the kite. He shook out the lovely long tail.

The wind caught hold of the kite and pulled at it in delight. John threw it up into the air. At once it rose high, and higher still as John let out more and more string. It quivered and shook like a live thing. Its lovely tail swung below it, twisting and shaking. It was marvellous!

"Oh, Annie! Doesn't the kite fly beautifully?" cried John, pleased. "It's the best kite in the world! Oh, look, it's pulling so hard at my hand that it feels like a horse wanting to gallop away!"

"Well, hold on tight," said Annie. "It would be dreadful if you let go and it flew away by itself! Hold on tight!"

All the toys watched in amazement. Could this really be the poor quiet kite they had so often laughed at? The kite that had no legs and couldn't play with them? The kite whom they had teased and tangled? They couldn't believe it! It was flying higher and higher in the air, sometimes dipping down in great circles, sometimes flapping its tail in glee. It was lovely to watch.

"Would you believe that the quiet old kite could fly like that?" said the red-haired doll.

"*I* couldn't fly up in the air," said the teddy.

"It's much, much cleverer than we are," said the train.

The little white ostrich was proud of

her fine friend. She watched out of her black eyes and wondered if the kite would bump into the big white clouds that raced along so fast.

At last the wind dropped and the kite swooped down. It lay quietly on the grass. John heard his mother calling and turned to Annie. "Come on – that's Mum. She has some biscuits for us!"

The children raced indoors. Soon the wind began to blow again and the kite lifted itself a little from the grass. "Ostrich," it called, "climb on to my tail! I'll take you flying! You are a nice little bird and you ought to try how lovely it is to fly through the air!"

"Ostriches don't fly. They only run!" called the teddy bear, jealously. He would so very much have loved to climb on to the end of the kite's tail himself.

"This ostrich is going to fly!" said the little white ostrich, and she settled herself on the very end of the kite's tail. There came a great gust of wind and the kite rose up joyously. It flew up in to the air, dragging its long tail behind it. And on the end flew the little white ostrich half delighted, half frightened, but enjoying herself thoroughly.

"The kite will fly away and John will be cross," said the teddy. But the kite didn't because John had been wise enough to tie the end of its string to a post. So when the kite rose very high it had to stay there, because the string was tied fast to the post and the kite couldn't get away.

Soon John and Annie came out with their biscuits. "Look!" cried John. "My kite is flying itself. Isn't it clever!"

When he pulled down the kite to put it away, John had such a surprise. He called to Annie.

"Annie! Look! Your little white ostrich has been flying on the tail of the kite! Isn't that strange?"

When the kite was put away in the toy cupboard that night, the toys came up to it. They felt ashamed.

"Kite, you were marvellous today," said the red-haired doll.

"Kite, I'm sorry I tangled your string," said the bear. "I didn't know how important your string was to you."

"It's quite all right," the kite said generously. "I know I'm quiet and dull when I'm lying here doing nothing, but I'm a different fellow, I can tell you, when I'm up in the air!"

"Give the others a ride on your tail next time," said the little white ostrich, who was pleased to find that the toys were being nice to her friend.

"I will!" said the kite. And it'll keep its word, no doubt about that. I'd love to see the red-haired doll swinging on the end of its tail, wouldn't you?

Lazy Little Pimmy

Pimmy was the pixie who lived in Pimmy Cottage at the end of Snapdragon village. You could tell he was lazy because his garden was full of weeds, his windows were dirty, and his gate hung crookedly.

Now, one day it was very, very windy. Pimmy put on his red hat with the feather in it and went out. It was a silly hat to wear on a windy day, but Pimmy liked it very much. It was his best hat, and the feather made him feel grand.

The wind saw Pimmy's hat in delight. *Whooooo!* Just the kind of hat the wind liked to play with. It swept down on Pimmy, swished off his hat, and made it sail high in the air.

"Oh – bother, bother, bother!" cried Pimmy, as he saw his lovely hat whirled away by the wind. "Come back hat!"

But the hat didn't. It was enjoying itself. It sailed off, went over a tree, and then came down on the top of the shed in Dame Stern's garden.

"That's a nuisance," said Pimmy, screwing up his nose. "I daren't go and get my hat off Dame Stern's shed without asking her – and she may snap my head off, she's so bad-tempered."

Anyway, he went to ask if he might get it, because he really couldn't bear to lose such a lovely hat. He knocked on Dame Stern's door.

"If it's the washing, leave it on the step!" called a voice.

"It isn't," said Pimmy.

"Well, if it's the paper-boy, bring me the right paper tomorrow, or I'll chase you all the way down the street and back again," said the voice.

Pimmy felt glad he wasn't the paper-boy.

"It isn't the paper-boy," he said. "It's Pimmy. My hat has been blown on top of your shed, Dame Stern, and please may I get it?"

"No, you may not," said Dame Stern. "You'll fall off and break your neck."

"I could climb up a ladder all right," Pimmy said politely.

"I haven't got a ladder," said Dame Stern. "But Old Man Stamper has. You might be able to borrow his."

Pimmy went off to Old Man Stamper's house. The old fellow was in his garden, digging.

"Please, Mr Stamper, could you lend me your ladder?" said Pimmy. "My hat's blown on to the top of Dame Stern's shed."

"What a silly hat to have," said Old

Man Stamper. "Well – I'll lend you my ladder, but you must do something for me first. You run along to Mother Grumble's and ask her to let me have a little of her cough medicine. My cough's so bad at night."

Pimmy didn't want to go to Mother Grumble's. It was a long way to go, and he was afraid of her. But still, he wouldn't get the ladder if he didn't, and if he didn't get the ladder, he'd lose his hat. So he had to go.

He came to Mother Grumble's and knocked at the door. He could hear the old lady grumbling away to someone.

"And if it isn't one thing, it's another.

One of my hens got loose this morning, and it pecked up all my lettuce, and then a stray dog came and dug up my carrot bed, and . . ."

Pimmy knocked again.

"And now here's someone come to the door, just as I've got settled down to have a cup of tea! Really, if it isn't one thing, it's another. Who's at the door? Speak up!"

"Pimmy the pixie!" called Pimmy. "Please will you let Old Man Stamper have some of your cough medicine?"

"Well, if he isn't asking for something or other all day long!" said Mother Grumble. "First it's a pinch of tea, then it's a box of matches, and now it's cough medicine. I haven't got a bottle to put some in for him. You'd better go and ask the chemist to let you have one, Pimmy. Then I'll give you some."

Pimmy groaned. The chemist lived over the other side of the hill. He set off again and came to the chemist's.

"Hello, lazy little Pimmy," said the chemist, who had once had Pimmy for an errand boy and sent him away because he was so lazy. "What do you want?"

"Could you let me have an old medicine bottle for Mother Grumble?" said Pimmy.

"Ah, you want something for nothing, do you?" said the chemist. "No, no – if you want a bottle, you must do something to get it, Pimmy. I don't give something for nothing!"

"Well, what shall I do?" said Pimmy, feeling that he would never get home that day.

"See this parcel?" said the chemist. "Well, you take it to Mrs Flap's for me,

and when you come back you shall have the bottle. See?"

Pimmy set off. Mrs Flap's house was half a mile away. Pimmy wished he had had his shoes mended the week before, as he should have done. There was a hole in one, and the stones kept coming in and hurting his foot.

He came to Mrs Flap's. Nobody answered the door. Pimmy knocked and knocked, more and more loudly. Then the window of the next house flew up, and an angry face looked out.

"What's all this noise? It sounds like a thousand postmen at the door – knock, knock, knock! Mrs Flap's not in. She's out shopping."

"Oh dear," said Pimmy, looking at the angry face of Mr Glum. "I've come so far to bring her a parcel from the chemist."

"Well, I'll take it in for you if you'll do something for me," said Mr Glum. "My dog hasn't been for his walk today and he's longing for it. My leg's bad and I can't take him. You just take him round

the streets and back again, and when you come back I'll take the parcel in for Mrs Flap. Then you won't need to sit on her doorstep and wait."

"I don't like taking dogs for walks," said Pimmy. "And besides, I'm tired."

Mr Glum looked at him hard. "Ah, you're lazy little Pimmy, aren't you?" he said. "You wouldn't take a dog for a walk, no matter how hard he begged you, would you? You're too lazy."

He slammed down his window. Pimmy stared at it in despair. Mrs Flap might be hours before she came back from her shopping. He couldn't wait all that time. He would have to take Mr Glum's dog for a walk, even though his legs felt dreadfully tired.

So he shouted out loudly, "Mr Glum, Mr Glum, I'll take your dog out!"

The front door opened. Mr Glum limped out with a very large dog on a lead. "Here you are," he said. "Take him for a nice run and come back again."

Pimmy took the lead and set off. He meant to go round the corner and sit down for ten minutes, and then take the dog home again. But the dog had other ideas.

Pimmy didn't take that dog for a run – it took Pimmy for a gallop. It was a large dog and a strong dog, and a very

determined dog. It tore off down the street and Pimmy was dragged after it.

"Here! Hi! Whoa!" panted Pimmy. But the dog took not the slightest notice. It rushed on like an express train and Pimmy had to follow it. He ran and he ran and he panted and he puffed. He had never in his life run so fast.

Then the dog suddenly turned and ran back to sniff an exciting smell. The lead wound itself round Pimmy's legs, and he sat down very suddenly. The dog looked surprised and sniffed at Pimmy's ear.

"Don't do that, you horrid dog," panted Pimmy. "What do you mean by rushing off at top speed like that? Don't sniff in my ear – it tickles."

The dog sniffed at Pimmy's nose. Pimmy got up, and the dog at once started off at top speed again. But, luckily, this time it made for home. Pimmy tore along behind it, almost falling over his own feet.

He got back to Mr Glum's, his face hot and red, his breath coming in such loud pants that Mr Glum heard him before he even saw him. Mr Glum smiled one of his rare smiles.

"I see Scamper has been giving you a good run," he said. "Well, it will do you good, lazy little Pimmy. Here, here, Scamper! Come in. Where is the parcel you wanted me to give to Mrs Flap? Ah, there she is. You can give it to her yourself now."

He shut his door; Pimmy glared at it. So he had taken that dreadful dog out for nothing! He scowled, gave the parcel to Mrs Flap, and set off wearily to the chemist's.

"What a long time you've been!" said the chemist. "Lazy as usual, I suppose – just crawled along, didn't you?"

"I've been rushing along at about sixty miles an hour!" Pimmy said crossly, and he took the bottle the chemist held out to him. "Thank you. If I'd known how many miles I'd have to run when I took that parcel for you, I wouldn't have done it!"

Pimmy took the bottle to Mother

Grumble. She got up to fill it, grumbling away as usual. "If it isn't one thing, it's another. No sooner do I sit myself down than up I have to get again for lazy little fellows like you, Pimmy!"

Pimmy took the bottle of cough medicine to Old Man Stamper. The old man was very glad to have it. He took a dose at once.

"Could I borrow your ladder, please?" said Pimmy. "You said I could if I brought you some cough medicine."

"Dear me, I'd forgotten," said Old Man Stamper. "There it is, look. Mind you bring it back."

Pimmy took the ladder. It was heavy. He staggered back to Dame Stern's garden.

"Oh, you've got the ladder, have you?" said Dame Stern. "Now you be careful not to tread on any of my beds, Pimmy!"

Pimmy was very careful. His arms ached with the heavy ladder and he was glad to put it up against the shed. He went up. Now at last, at last, he would get his lovely hat!

But it wasn't there! It was gone! Pimmy burst into tears. Dame Stern was surprised.

"What's the matter?" she called. "Oh, of course, your hat is gone. Yes, I saw it go. The wind came down and swept it away. I don't know where it went to."

Pimmy cried bitterly. He carried the heavy ladder back to Old Man Stamper. Then he went home, still crying. And when he got there, what did he see in his very own garden but his lovely hat, feather and all!

"Oh – who brought you back?" he cried in delight, and put it on. The wind swept round him and shouted in his ear.

"I brought it back here, Pimmy. I was just playing a trick on you, that's all. I brought it back!"

"Oh, you mean, unkind wind!" cried Pimmy. "I've borrowed a heavy ladder and carried it here – I've fetched cough medicine – I've carried a parcel – and I've taken a dog out for a run – all to get my hat, and now it's here! I'm tired out!"

"Do you good, do you good, lazy little Pimmy!" said the wind, and tried to pull his hat off again. "Do you good! Whoooo-ooo-ooo!"

A Lame Duck and
a Stile

"I'm taking my doll for a walk, Mummy," said Amanda. "I've put her into her pram and tucked her up. We shall just go across the fields and back."

"You won't be able to take your pram over the stile," said her mother, "so don't try."

"I won't," said Amanda. "I'll just walk as far as the stile, then I'll turn back. That will be a nice walk for Rosebud."

Rosebud was her doll, a small, lovely little thing, lying in the pram with her eyes shut. She always shut them when she lay down. Mother said she wished babies would do that too. It would be so nice if they all went to sleep as soon as they were put down in prams or cots!

Rosebud opened her eyes when she sat

up. She had blue eyes and golden hair. Amanda loved her very much. She liked taking her for walks in the pram. She often talked to her as she went along.

She talked to her that morning, although Rosebud was asleep, with her eyes shut.

"It's a lovely sunny day," said Amanda. "The buttercups are out all over the field, Rosebud. They are brushing against the wheels of the pram and making them all yellow."

Rosebud said nothing. She kept her eyes shut.

"The birds are singing," said Amanda. "I can hear them. Sit up and listen, Rosebud. It would do you good to be awake now."

She sat Rosebud up. Rosebud opened her blue eyes and looked at Amanda. She was always smiling, and her smile showed two rows of tiny white teeth. Amanda sometimes tried to clean Rosebud's tiny teeth, but it wasn't easy.

"Now you can see the buttercups and hear the birds singing," said Amanda.

Then she stopped talking and looked puzzled.

"What's that noise?" she said. "It sounds like a very loud quacking!"

It was. "Quack, quack, quack!" went the noise. "Quack, quack, QUACK!"

"There aren't any ducks near here, surely," said Amanda. "They all swim on the pond at the farm. Rosebud, we had better find out if it is a duck."

They went on down the path across the buttercup field. The noise grew louder. Amanda came to the stile and stopped.

The quacking seemed to come from the other side. She peeped over the stile. She was surprised to see a large white duck there, looking up at her out of bright eyes.

"Hello!" said Amanda, rather startled. "What are you quacking for?"

"QUACK!" said the duck, and put its head through an opening under the stile.

"I see. You want to get over that stile," said Amanda. "Well, why don't you?"

"Quack, quack," said the duck, in a sad sort of voice. Amanda saw that it had a bad foot. It had webbed skin between its toes to help it when it swam – but the webbing on one foot was torn. Now it was lame and could hardly get along on its one good foot.

"Poor thing! You can't get over the stile!" said Amanda, in pity. "I'll help you over. Mummy is always saying something about helping lame ducks over a stile, but I never thought I should do that! I thought it was just a saying that meant helping people in trouble."

But this time it was real. There was a real lame duck, trying to get over a real stile, and Amanda was there to help it.

She climbed over the stile, and tried to push the duck through, over the bottom bar. It was difficult because the duck didn't seem to think that Amanda was trying to help it. It gave her a peck.

"Oh, don't do that when I'm trying to help you!" said Amanda. "That's not kind. Now – one more push – and over you go, poor lame duck!"

This time the duck did go over the stile and, much to its surprise, found itself on the other side. This was where it wanted to be.

It had swum out of the pond and down the stream. Then it had caught its foot on some sharp stones, and climbed on to the bank because its foot hurt it too much to swim. It thought it would go home by the fields. But it hadn't been able to get over the stile.

Now it was over. It looked up at Amanda and said "Quack!" She thought perhaps it meant "Thank you". It began to waddle slowly along the path, which led to the farm where its pond was. But it couldn't even waddle properly now. Its foot hurt it too much.

It sank down among the buttercups and gave a most doleful quack. Amanda looked at it in alarm.

"Can't you walk? You ought to get back to the farm and have your leg seen to. Try again."

The duck tried again, but once more it fell over. Amanda couldn't bear it. She wondered what to do.

"I know!" she said. "I'll wheel you in my pram. I once read a story about a little girl who wheeled a lost lamb home in her pram. So I don't see why I shouldn't wheel a lame duck."

She bent down to pick up the big, heavy duck. It pecked her hands.

"Don't!" said Amanda. "I'm only trying to help you! I can't leave you here. The fox might get you! He lives about these fields."

She bent down again, and again the

duck pecked her and made a nasty sound in its throat. Amanda didn't know what to do. What an ungrateful duck!

She had one last try. She picked up the big duck and popped it into her pram! It pecked her again and tried to strike her with its wing. Amanda felt rather hurt.

"You're unkind," she said. "Oh, do keep still! You're sitting on poor Rosebud!"

The duck wriggled about in the pram,

and then it pecked Rosebud's nose! Amanda was really cross.

"Now look here, Duck, I've done a lot for you, and I'm taking you home in Rosebud's pram. You've quacked at me and pecked me, and hit me with your wing – but you're not going to peck Rosebud! Sit still!"

After that the duck did sit still. It squatted down comfortably in the pram, leaving Rosebud just enough room, and quacked no more. It closed its eyes.

"Perhaps it likes being in the pram," thought Amanda, and wheeled it carefully along the path. She came to the farm and called to the farmer's wife.

"I've got one of your ducks in my pram. It has hurt its foot."

"Bless us all! Fancy wheeling it back here, you kind little thing!" cried Mrs Straw, and hurried to get the duck. It gave Amanda one last peck.

"It doesn't like me," said Amanda, almost in tears. "I only tried to help it. It keeps pecking me."

"Only because it is in pain, dear," said

Mrs Straw, and took the duck away to see to its foot. "Thank you for bringing it home."

Amanda went home with Rosebud to tell her mother about the duck. "It wasn't a nice duck," she said. "It didn't like me, even when I tried to help it. It never even quacked a thank-you."

Amanda was sad. She went to her pram to take Rosebud out – and then she got a surprise!

In the pram lay a big greenish-grey duck's egg! Amanda stared at it in the greatest astonishment. She picked it up and ran to her mother.

"Mummy! The duck's laid me an egg! It must have liked me after all! Look!"

"What a beauty!" said her mother. "That's the best reward the duck could give you, isn't it? You can have it for your breakfast."

"But I don't like duck's eggs," said Amanda. "I had one at Auntie's once and it tasted funny. I don't want to eat it, Mummy . . ."

"Well, shall we give it to Henny-Penny to sit on?" said Mother. "She has ten of her own eggs to sit on, and she won't mind if we add this duck's egg to her batch. Then maybe you will have a little duckling of your own!"

Amanda thought that was a fine idea. She put the warm duck's egg with Henny-Penny's big batch of brown eggs.

Henny-Penny, the brown hen, didn't seem to mind a bit.

And do you know, out of that greenish-grey duck's egg came the dearest little yellow duckling you ever saw! Henny-Penny sat on her eggs for some weeks, and ten of them hatched into yellow chicks – and one into the duckling!

"It's my duckling!" cried Amanda, in delight. "My very own. You shall be my pet, little duckling. I shall call you Quack!"

I saw Quack yesterday, and Amanda told me this story. She thought you might like to hear it too.

"I helped a lame duck over a stile!" she said, "and that's how I got a duckling for my own. I am a lucky girl, aren't I?"

Let's Pass
It On!

Susan's mother was very kind. She was always helping people, and everyone was very fond of her. But when anyone said, "Oh, Mrs Timms, do tell me something I can do for you in return," what do you think she said?

She said, "Oh, don't bother about that. Just pass it on!"

"Mummy, what do you mean when you tell people to pass it on?" said Susan one day. "Pass what on?"

"My bit of kindness!" said her mother. "I don't want people to pay back my kindness to me, Susan – but I would like them to pass it on to somebody else!"

"Oh, I see, Mummy," said Susan, and she smiled. "What a good idea! You do somebody a kindness, and then you say

'Pass it on' so that perhaps that person does another kindness, and says 'Pass it on' again – and the bit of kindness goes on and on and on."

"Yes," said Mother. "It's a very good idea, isn't it? The world would be full of kindness if only everyone said 'Pass it on'."

"I shall do it too," said Susan. "Mummy, do something kind for me, and say 'Pass it on', will you?"

"Right," said her mother. "I shall mend your poor old broken doll for you. Where is she?"

Susan gave her mother the doll and

her mother set to work to mend it. It took her a long time, but the doll looked lovely when she had finished.

"There you are, darling," she said to Susan.

"Thank you for your kindness, Mummy," said Susan.

"Just pass it on," said her mother at once. And so that bit of kindness started its trip.

Susan passed it on. She met old Mrs Down in the road, carrying a very heavy bag. "Let me carry it!" said Susan, and took it out of the old lady's hand.

She carried it all the way home for her, and it made her arm very tired. "Thank you," said Mrs Down. "I shall give you a present for that bit of kindness."

"No, thank you," said Susan at once. "Just pass it on, will you?"

"Well, what a lovely idea," said Mrs Down. "I certainly will!"

So she waited for a chance to pass on the bit of kindness. It soon came. Mr Dick went by, limping, for he had a bad leg. Mrs Down said good morning to him,

and asked him where he was going.

"I've got to walk all the way into the town and back for some bread – and my leg is so bad this morning," he said.

"Don't you bother to do that now!" said Mrs Down. "I've a bit of kindness to pass on today. I can give you a loaf of bread."

So she did, and Mr Dick was so glad. "Now don't you thank me for that," said Mrs Down. "Just pass it on, Mr Dick, pass it on!"

Mr Dick went back home. He went

into his house and cut himself some bread-and-butter, thinking of Mrs Down's kindness which made him feel nice and warm. He wondered how he could pass it on.

A little girl came to the door, looking very shy, for she was afraid of Mr Dick, who was often cross.

"Please," she said, "my ball has fallen in your garden. Can I get it?"

"Certainly, certainly!" said Mr Dick. "I'll come and help you find it, and look, here is an apple for you!"

"Oh, thank you," said the little girl

and gave him such a smile that Mr Dick felt warm all over again. "You are kind."

"Now listen before you go," said Mr Dick. "You've got to pass this bit of kindness on, see? Don't forget. It's a bit of kindness that is going round."

"I'll pass it on," said the little girl, quite pleased to join in the game. She ran home with her ball and her apple. When she got home her mother called her.

"Katie! I know you want to play, but I need some butter. Could you go and get me some?"

Katie remembered the bit of kindness she had to pass on. "I'll go now," she said, and off she went. Her mother was pleased with her.

"That's a kind little girl," she said when Katie came back.

"Mummy, please pass the bit of kindness on," said Katie, and told her mother about Mr Dick. Her mother smiled.

"I'll certainly pass it on," she said, and wondered how she could. "I know!" she said, "I'll go and take some books and ice cream to little Jack Brown today. You shall come with me. He's been so ill, poor little chap. He will like some visitors."

"That's a lovely big bit of kindness, isn't it," said Katie, joyfully. They set off with the ice cream and some books that afternoon, and dear me, Jack was so pleased to see them. He ate the ice cream while they were there.

"You're very, very kind," he said. "I wish I could pay you back somehow."

"No, don't," said Katie's mother. "Pass the bit of kindness on, will you? That's what we're doing – passing it on!"

Jack thought and thought how he could, but it was difficult to do much in the way of kindness when he was in bed. When he got up, he looked about for a way to pass on the bit of kindness, and he soon found it. He suddenly saw somebody hurrying to catch a bus drop a glove in the road.

He went and picked it up. "I know where she lives!" thought Jack. "But, oh, dear, what a long way away. Still, it's

a good way of passing on the bit of
kindness, so I must do it. I'll walk there
now. I know the lady will be glad to have
this nice leather glove back."

So off he went. He was rather tired
after his illness, but he didn't stop till
he got to the house.

It was my house, and it was my glove!
I was pleased to have it back. "You are a
kind little boy," I said. "What can I do for
you in return?"

"Please just pass the bit of kindness

on," said Jack. "That's all I want."

Well, well – how was I to do that? "I know!" I said. "I will sit down and write a story about it for all the children I know – and if they think it's kind of me to tell them the story, I shall say to them, "Well, pass on the bit of kindness, please, that Susan started. Keep it going!"

So pass it on, will you, this very day – and don't forget to give the message: Pass it on!